GOING ALL IN

KATE CAMPFIELD

ALSO BY KATE CAMPFIELD

Letting it Ride

Calling Your Bluff

Upping the Ante

GOING ALL IN

GOING ALL IN

KATE CAMPFIELD

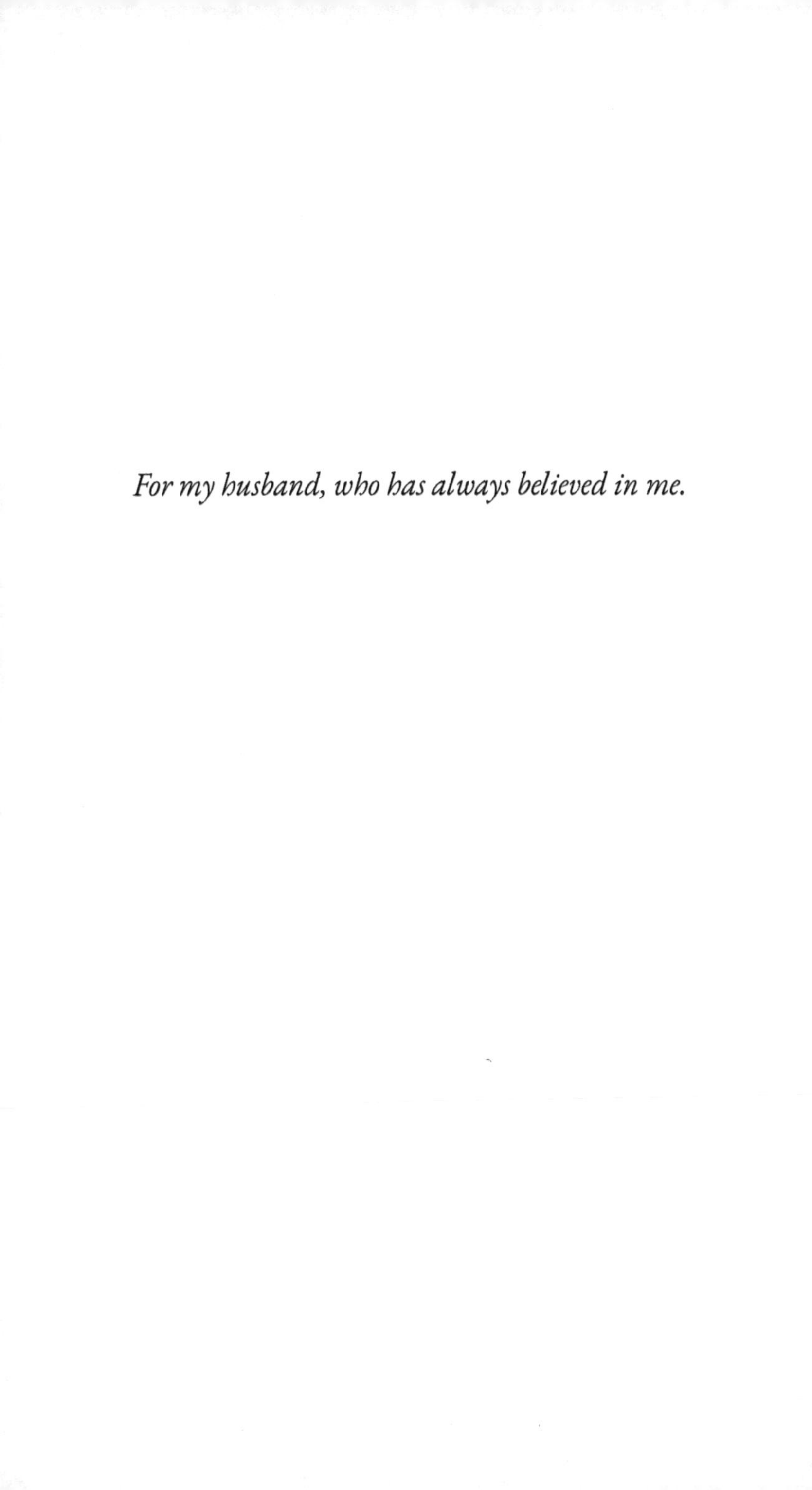

For my husband, who has always believed in me.

CONTENTS

1

—————

HOLLY

I'm late, but what else is new?

You'd think after my night of hot, life-altering sex with Maddox, I'd be different some-how, but nope, still the same hot mess.

It's Friday evening, and I'm rushing home from work as usual, but instead of getting ready to go out with my roommate, I have approximately thirteen minutes to get ready for dinner. I'm meeting my dad at a restaurant in Rittenhouse.

It's not his usual scene—or mine—but I've been looking forward to a meal at the swanky steakhouse for days. Fancy restaurants expect you to be on time for reservations, though, and I'm cutting it close.

I brush out my dark hair and twist it into a simple updo, then add a swipe of blush to my cheeks. I've changed into my go-to little black dress, which is, of course, JJ's dress that she let me use. That's one of the reasons we've been roommates so long: we wear the same size, and living together doubles both our closets, or at least it doubles mine.

JJ's clothes are typically more fashionable and revealing than even the simple things I buy, so it's usually *me* borrowing *her* stuff. But if she ever wants to wear a pair of khakis or a sensible wrap dress, I've got her covered.

I paw through the makeup that's littered across the cracked laminate counter, looking for eyeliner and ignoring the hairbrush that skitters off the counter and to the floor. Crap. I don't even have time to pick it up, so I leave it there for now.

My phone buzzes with a text and I curse under my breath. In all likelihood, it's JJ asking me to go to the bar with her. She knows I'm having dinner with my dad, right? I'm pretty sure I told her, and she's aware that time with my dad is sacred. I'm willing to go along with her plans most of the time; after all, she's the extrovert here who adopted me as her introvert sidekick back in grad school—reason number two we're best friends. But tonight, she's on her own.

Maybe it's another text from that guy I met at the

bar the other night. JJ and I went to Darby's, which was our favorite bar during grad school.

I remember it being all fun and exciting, not loud and sticky like it seems to be now. The one redeeming spot of the night was meeting the guy. Maddox, the guy who gave me orgasms like I've never known before. I should check to see if the text is from him.

Shit. Or it could be work.

I swipe the phone open while I add some mascara. I know, work-life balance and all that, but I can't turn off my social worker brain. There's always the chance that some kid needs me, and for me, that always comes first.

DAD

Got here early. We're sitting in the back. Take your time.

I blow out a breath of relief that it's not work, followed by a small gasp of panic. He's at the restaurant already? Crap.

At least it's not work.

I put my favorite silver earrings on and hop across the living room while I pull on my heels one at a time.

It's only when I make it down to the lobby to wait for my Uber that I think to wonder why he said *we're* waiting. Is he with someone else?

The ride across the bridge to Rittenhouse is quick, and I scroll through my phone while we're driving, re-reading some of the texts from my one-night stand that might be more.

Maddox might have potential. I'm not like JJ, who always has someone on her arm, or at least in her bed. I haven't actually dated since Jared, and that was three years ago. But there's something about this guy. His quiet confidence, his engaging smile.

Between that, the two vodka cranberries I had, and the fact that it's almost Christmas again, the vibes all mixed together with my emotions made me think it was a good idea to go home with him.

And fuck, was it hot.

I don't do things like that, not ever. I make careful decisions about who I date. I get to know them before I go home with them. I go out with respectable, upstanding guys. Ones who don't have the potential to humiliate me, especially in front of family, the way Jared did.

Memories swirl up around me, as cold and icy as the day of my mom's funeral, before I can push them back down where they belong.

Maddox might just be a keeper. Let's think about that instead. The off-the-charts steam of our night aside, he's been texting me every morning.

Every. Single. Morning.

Just something simple: a *good morning* or a *hope you slept well* or a *have a good day at work*. But it's enough to let me know he's thinking about me, and we've only had that one night.

The Uber pulls to a stop at the curb. I thank my driver, then jump out and smooth my dress as I walk up to the restaurant entrance, walking as fast as I can in these heels without falling down. This place is fancy enough that they have the carpet on the sidewalk, and it's working in my favor right now, keeping me from slipping on the icy pavement.

I tell the hostess that I'm meeting someone, and she directs me to a table in the back.

I maneuver around the carefully spaced tables, all set with white linen tablecloths and wineglasses. In the dim lighting, I spot my dad across the room and raise my hand to wave before I realize he's not with someone. He's with two someones actually, both of them seated with their backs to me, at a table with five place settings. One, a woman with brown hair streaked with gray, and the other a man with dark brown hair that's cropped close and broad shoulders. As I walk closer, I can see a bit of the short beard that lines an angular jaw.

My dad finally sees me and returns my wave when I'm near enough to talk. The other two turn around in greeting, and my heart jolts in my chest.

The woman is someone I've never met. She looks like she's about my dad's age, with laugh lines that crease her soft skin. But that's not what makes me stop short.

It's that the man sitting next to her is Maddox.

My heart beats faster and my breath comes in shallow pants as I realize that it's the same man who's been inside me, who's had my nipples in his mouth. The guy I was supposed to go on a first official date with tomorrow night.

And he's sitting across from my father.

The woman has stood from her chair and swooped me into a hug, saving me momentarily. "Holly! It's so nice to meet you." Her scent envelops me as she holds me tight against her soft body, notes of elegant jasmine and rose.

It takes me a few seconds to get my body to function again after my brain completely misfires at seeing

Maddox here, but the physical contact—albeit from a woman I've never met—helps to snap me out of my daze. I bring my arms around her, returning the hug, and she finally releases me.

"I'm Judy. Your dad has told me so much about you." She keeps her hands on my shoulders and holds me at arm's length.

Am I supposed to know who she is? My dad never told me he knows someone named Judy, let alone who in the world she is to him.

"It's... nice to meet you," I manage.

My dad clears his throat. Judy drops her hands and motions to the empty seat next to my dad.

I slide into it, finally making eye contact with Maddox. He lifts an eyebrow and smiles. Does he have any clue what's going on here?

"This is Maddox, Judy's son." My dad motions to Maddox.

I nod in... something. Greeting? Acknowledgement? Confusion?

All my brain can think is, *I've seen him naked.*

My dad is completely oblivious to my mental state for once in his life. "She has two daughters, too. One lives in Boston, so she's not here tonight, and... there's Addison."

A woman who looks to be about my age

approaches the table, tossing long red hair over her shoulder. She looks just as confused as I am, so at least I'm not the only one in the dark. "Hi, Mom. Maddox. And..."

Judy introduces my dad and I, and the woman slides into the last empty seat at the table, studying Dad and me with interest.

My dad clears his throat again, even though no one else is talking. It's always been his way of getting the attention of a room or setting up for a big announcement. As usual, it works, all of us silently looking to him. "So, kids. Judy and I wanted to have dinner with you all tonight to share some news."

Judy and I. Like they're a team.

I finally make eye contact with Maddox, whose brow is wrinkled. So, he has no clue, either. What are they...

My dad is reaching across the table. He's taking Judy's hand. They're smiling at each other, like—

"Judy and I are getting married."

My gaze falls to Judy's hand, the one that's touching my dad's. There's a diamond solitaire on her left ring finger.

"Mom? That's amazing! Congratulations!" Addie is the first to react. She jumps out of her chair and hugs her mom, then my dad, then me. "I'm so excited to be getting another sister!"

That's when I make eye contact with Maddox, and it hits me. *Sister.* That means that Maddox is about to be my...

No.

I manage to hold it together while Addison chatters away, her excited questions for Dad and Judy monopolizing the conversation. Once we place our orders, I excuse myself, beelining for the bathroom. I lock myself in a stall and lean against the wall, focusing on my breathing like I teach my foster kids to do when they're feeling overwhelmed.

In, one, two, three. Out, one, two, three.

But when I close my eyes, I just find myself reliving that night with Maddox.

"Can I get you a drink?" The deep voice resonates in my ear.

I turn back to the bar, ready to tell the bartender exactly what I think of his service so far, but he's still at the other end of the counter where he's spent the last twenty minutes.

There's a man leaned up against the bar next to me, his eyebrows raised like he's looking for an answer.

And he's a man. Not a man-child, like these post-college kids.

Dark brown hair. Eyes that are so dark they're almost black. They're hypnotic. A well-maintained beard over his defined chin that indicates an adequate amount of testosterone and an appropriate amount of attention to self-grooming.

The man smiles at me, the lines at the corners of his eyes creasing. Swoon. It's one of the things I look for in guys, and fuck, this guy has them in spades. It's some-thing most college guys don't have, with their limited life experience and overzealous sunscreen use. It's a marker of maturity and that someone has spent a lot of time smiling in a genuine way.

"What would you like?" He's still smiling— eye lines and all— and ignoring the fact that I've been staring at him silently.

I blink and try to recover before he realizes I might be a lost cause. "Oh. Um. I'll take a vodka cranberry, but I think it'll be a while. The bartender hasn't come down here in forever."

He offers me a nod. Then, I swear to God, with one

flick of his wrist, the bartender is headed our way, his attention firmly on this guy. While his attention is on the bartender, I take the opportunity to run my gaze over the rest of his body. Dark-wash jeans fit him perfectly, hugging a waist that looks solid. A long-sleeve grey Henley wraps over wide shoulders.

"What can I get for you?" the bartender asks, offering us a pleasant smile like he hasn't just avoided this side of the room for twenty minutes.

To be fair, he's asking the mystery guy, not me.

"I'll take whatever IPA is on tap. And a vodka cranberry for..." My new companion trails off, looking at me.

Oh. Now they're both looking at me.

I try to remember my own name. Jesus, a hot guy looks at me, and my brain misfires. "Holly. Thank you."

The bartender flashes a grin. "Like, happy holly-days?"

I offer him the same fake smile that I give anyone who brings up the holidays. "Kinda."

The bartender gives me a brief nod, correctly sensing that I'm not in the mood to talk about the origins of my name, and moves away to grab our drinks.

Mystery Guy turns his attention fully to me. "Nice to meet you. Holly is a pretty name. Seems perfect for the holidays, huh?"

"I guess." I'd like to get away from the topic of the holidays and Christmas.

Because if you must know, then yes, I'm a Christmas time baby. My birthday is on December 26th.

My mom used to say that Santa was just a bit late with his gift that year. Christmas used to be a big deal for us. My mom would go all out with decorations, leave notes from Santa and the Elf on the Shelf, sprinkle glitter and leave reindeer paw prints in the snow on Christmas morning.

When she died, it was like the magic died with her.

Before I can alienate this guy further—or ask him his name—he turns away from me to pick up the glass of beer that the bartender sets in front of him, his shirt stretching tight against his muscles as he reaches. He slides the reddish cocktail my way before he sets a bill on the bar and slides it across, ignoring the beer residue.

I bring the drink to my lips and take a sip, keeping my eyes on him.

The drink is the perfect amount of tart and sweet, and I can actually taste the vodka in this one, which means it's stronger than the weak-ass first one I got my hands on. This mystery guy really does have special powers over bartenders; he can command attention and strong drinks. Amazing.

"I'm Maddox." Mystery Guy holds a hand out to me.

I do my breathing exercises again and leave the stall, checking my makeup in the mirror as I wash my hands. Obviously, dating Maddox now is out of the question. My family would never let approve of the whole stepbrother thing. And after *The Incident*, I'm not giving them any more reason to judge me.

2

MADDOX

Addison is doing what she does best—talking—and no one seems to mind when I slip away from the table to follow Holly to the bathrooms.

I wait for her in the hallway between the two restrooms. When she emerges, her face is a mask of calm until she sees me. Then her brows pinch together, and her lips press into a thin line.

"What are you doing here?" she says, her voice sharper than I remember, but then what I'm remembering best are her breathy moans as I drove into her.

"I came to see if you were okay. I know we talked about your mom passing, and how close you were with your dad. It seems like we were all caught off-guard by this engagement."

I'll start with that. We'll address the breathy moans later.

Holly and I had an amazing conversation that night last week. She caught my eye from across the bar, and there was something about her. Yeah, I know that's like the most cliché opening ever, but I honestly just wanted to buy her a drink and get to know her.

When we ended up talking over French fries and sodas at an all-night diner down the block from Darby's, the bar we were at, I was hooked.

Aside from her use of mayonnaise and hot sauce as a condiment, of course. There was no excuse for that. Ketchup is fine for French fries. More than fine, if you ask me. Ketchup is the ultimate condiment. I'll defend it to my dying day.

Anyway, what started as just sharing some late-night snacks turned into more. Her roommate had taken home a guy from the bar, something I gathered she does a lot, and I offered Holly a place to stay for the night so she didn't have walk in on them like she did the other time she told me about, when she startled a guy who slipped off the sofa, pulling the roommate down with him.

Apparently, the roommate hit her face on the coffee table, resulting in a black eye that she told everyone was a sex injury. I laughed so hard I almost snorted soda out of my nose.

That's the Holly I want. The girl who was laughing so hard she could barely get the story out. The wary creature who snapped a photo of my driver's license to send to said roommate before she agreed to stay with me. The confident woman who was the hottest sex I've had in years. Not this shell-shocked woman standing in front of me. I just want to gather her in my arms and kiss her until it's all better.

"It's... it's okay. I'm just surprised. We should get back." Holly pushes past me in the direction of the table, but I grab her arm.

"Holly. Talk to me."

She shakes her arm loose. "I'm not sure what there is to say, Maddox. I need to think."

I know she overthinks things. I can feel it happening right now. "We're still on for tomorrow night, though, right? We can talk more then, away from the family stuff."

She shakes her head, making my heart sink. "I-I need time, Maddox. Not tomorrow. Let me figure things out, and then we can talk."

Holly stalks away toward our table, narrowly avoiding Addison, who raises her eyebrows at me in an unspoken question.

I shake my head—*none of your business*—and follow Holly back to the table. I get the distinct sense that *needing time* means she's going to figure out all the reasons she shouldn't date me.

Should I care, after one night? Probably not. I usually don't. It's not like I bring girls back to my place often, but when I do, it's one night. Not even a whole night, usually. Giving her my number, asking her out for another night? This was way out on a limb for me, but when I crawled out here, it seemed like the right thing to do.

Now I feel like she's about to cut me off and send me crashing to the ground.

I look both ways as I cross the street with the phone pressed to my ear. "You should have seen her face. Shock, then horror, then this mask of calm. It was creepy, man."

"Maybe it was her reaction to you putting ketchup on an eighty-dollar steak." My best friend Cam laughs on the other end. "Or maybe you read her wrong. Who knows?"

"I didn't put ketchup on my steak, asshole. I can be classy when I need to be."

My place is twenty blocks away from the restaurant, but I needed the walk. The temperature has dropped from earlier in the day, and the frost is literally nipping at my nose. I caught a glimpse of myself in a storefront window. I look like Rudolph the Fucking Red-Nosed Reindeer.

"Maybe she's not happy about her dad getting remarried," Cam offers.

I blow out a breath that appears in a cloud of mist in the cold air. I want to believe him. "Maybe. I'll text her when I get home and my fingers work again." I flex them, trying to get the blood flowing. "It got fucking cold tonight, man."

"Good luck. Just don't do the Maddox thing until you have all the facts. You can give us the details tomorrow when we play." With that, he disconnects.

The Maddox Thing is what the guys have taken to calling my need to understand all possibilities and the likelihood of them occurring. Like with poker, most things have multiple possible outcomes, and each can be good or bad for each person involved. Like with poker, you can be dealt any hand to start, but the chances of certain combinations are limited. Knowing the probabilities and reading the players gives you an edge.

It's why I'm a damn good poker player. So good

that I've been able to do it for a living for a few years now, along with Cam and a few of our other friends. We review hands together, drive together to big tournaments. Poker is an individual game, but having buddies who understand and can help you improve is key.

My brain tends to look at card combinations, do the math, and ballpark the percentages of likelihood of winning a hand. I've never really understood how; it's just something I've always been able to do. It's been like this ever since I was little, when I took advantage of it to challenge kids on the playground to poker or blackjack. By the time I was twelve, I'd saved almost a thousand dollars that I'd won from schoolyard gambling.

It would be a cuter story if my mother hadn't found the bag of quarters and dollar bills and taken it away, putting it in a bank account for me with a lecture about taking advantage of other kids. At least she gave it back—with interest—when I graduated from college.

The point is, I like to know all the possibilities and their likelihood of occurring before I place my bets.

And in life, the possibilities are infinite, which is really fucking annoying.

I push the phone into my pocket and ball my

hands up for warmth. The air is so cold I can't smell the usual dirty scent of the city, which is a small blessing. However, the frigid air has done nothing to clear my mind. All it's done is sharpen my thoughts to clarify one thing: I like Holly. Like, really *like* her. I haven't been texting her every morning just for fun.

Is it the stepbrother thing that had her reeling tonight at dinner?

Maybe Cam is right, and she was just thrown off by the engagement announcement. Completely ignoring Cam's directive, I start to list each one of the possibilities in my head.

One. She's not ready to see her dad move on and was upset by the engagement. Seems like a reasonable conclusion.

Two. She doesn't like my mom with her dad. Fair, but who wouldn't love my mom? Everyone loves Judy. She's the entire reason some of my ex-girlfriends hung on as long as they did.

Three. She was planning on blowing me off until she saw me at dinner, and that screwed with her plans. Fuck, I don't like that one.

Four. She hates the idea of dating her future stepbrother.

Five. She thinks I kept the engagement from her on purpose.

Six.

I pause. So far, most of these possibilities would point to our relationship being doomed. In poker, when the overwhelming majority of possible outcomes are losses, you fold.

But even though I've only known Holly for a week, I'm absolutely sure of one thing.

I'm not folding. It may be the most ill-advised gamble I've ever made, and I may regret this. But I'm all in with this hand.

I'll give her tonight to cool off. But tomorrow morning, we're going to talk.

3

HOLLY

I bang on JJ's bedroom door. "THIS IS AN EMERGENCY."

She opens the door, clutching a blanket around her, blonde curls wild around her face. "This better be good, Holly. I'm in the middle of something."

Of course she is. It's Friday night.

"It is. Or rather, it's bad. Like, tequila bad."

JJ snaps into bestie mode immediately. She opens the door wider, revealing a guy lying on her bed. "Get out, Andy."

Five minutes later, Andy has vacated the premises and we're sitting on the living room floor with a pack of Oreos and a bottle of tequila. I take a shot directly from the bottle, wincing at the taste as I swallow.

"Start from the beginning. You said this is about a guy? How did you meet him?" JJ bites into an Oreo.

"At Darby's. Last week. Remember the guy I spent that one night with?"

She grins. "Oh, yeah! Mister One-Night Stand. You were kicking yourself for your loose morals or whatever all week." She grabs the bottle from me and takes a swig.

"Yeah. Maddox. We went to the diner and talked, and he's just... anyway." I clear my throat. "We were going to go out, like for real." I twist my Oreo apart to get to the cream.

JJ laughs. "It's so you to turn a one-night stand into a relationship."

I pause, the cookie halfway to my mouth. "It's not going to be a relationship."

"Why not? You like him, right? What happened since then?"

"My dad is getting married." I take the tequila bottle back. "Christmas Eve."

JJ's expression softens. "Oh, Holly. That's... it must be hard. No one will replace your mom. And Christmas Eve, too?"

That part of things occurred to me, but I haven't had time to focus on it. I haven't celebrated Christmas since Mom died. She died on December 2nd, and that was the year Christmas died, too. Dad and I didn't have the heart to pull out the Christmas things and celebrate without the woman who'd embodied the holiday for us for years.

And since then, Dad has just said that he'll be ready to celebrate the holidays when I am.

I never imagined him celebrating with a new family.

Judy seems to make him happy, and I want that for him. I really, really do. Dad and I weren't all that close while I was growing up, but since the accident, he and I have become a lot closer. Not the kind of friend you share tequila and Oreos with—that's JJ's department —but I've tried to spend more time with him, share more about my life.

Which is one reason why I feel so blindsided by this announcement, and also why I feel so shitty keeping things from him. But how do you broach that subject?

Oh, Maddox and I know one another already. We met at a bar, and by the end of that evening we were exchanging saliva.

I shake my head. "It's not that. His fiancée seems nice. Judy. She's really sweet. He seems happy." I take another sip of tequila. I'm going to regret this in the morning.

JJ looks perplexed, her eyes narrowed. "So what's the issue? Why are we sitting here killing your liver? What does this have to do with the guy?"

"Judy has kids," I mumble around the bottle that's still in my mouth.

"And?"

"And Maddox is her son." I close my eyes as I say it out loud.

JJ's expression hasn't changed. "So? I'm not seeing the issue here."

Having to spell it out makes it even worse.

"He's her *son*. The son of my future stepmother." I give her a significant look.

JJ trails off. "So that makes him…"

"Yeah. My future stepbrother."

JJ grabs the tequila bottle out of my hands and holds it out of my reach. "Hold on. You cock-blocked me to tell me that the guy you like is, at some point in the future, going to be your stepbrother? Why is that even an issue, Holly? People fuck their step siblings all the time. Remember Clueless?"

"That was a movie! And I'm not talking about what happens in those dirty books you read. I can't date my stepbrother. How would I even explain that to people? What would people think?" I reach for the alcohol, but she holds it further out of my grasp.

"It doesn't matter what people think. Get a grip."

I shake my head, sinking down onto the carpet. "You know I care. It just feels wrong. And it's not like we're actually dating, JJ."

She lowers the bottle and looks me pointedly in the eye. "Listen. You do you. If you want to date him, fuck what everyone else thinks. But if you don't want to pursue it with this new situation, that's fine too. I'm here for you no matter what, girl."

I let out a sigh. "I need a date for the wedding now, too."

JJ, ever the fixer, pulls out her phone. "That we can do."

"Oh my God. I'm so hungover." JJ shuffles into our shared office and flops onto the tattered sofa, which wheezes out a cloud of dust as she lands, laying an arm over her eyes.

It's a typical Monday. I'd be alarmed if this wasn't JJ's usual routine after she's been out all night. She's been this way since the very first time she dragged me to a bar that first week of grad school. Party hard, claim to have the worst hangover of your life and that you'll never drink again, and then go out that night and do it all over again.

I raise a brow. "Dramatic much? Anyway, that's what you get for taking some college kid home from the bar. You're almost thirty. We can't drink like we used to." I put my phone down to open the mini fridge between our desks and pull out the iced coffee I picked up for her. "Was the sex at least good?"

"He wasn't in college. And we're not almost thirty." JJ reaches out a hand for the cup without moving her arm from where it's draped over her eyes.

I press the coffee into her outstretched hand without responding.

A lesser friend would ignore the drama, but this is what you sign up for when your best friend is JJ. I choose not to point out that we are both, indeed, looking at the dubious landmark of our thirtieth birthdays within three years.

She sits up and practically chugs the coffee. "And... it happened."

"That good, huh?" I wrap my hands around my own mug, needing the warmth. How JJ can drink iced beverages when it's thirty-five degrees out, I've never understood.

JJ shrugs. "Yeah. That's about the best description I can give you of our coupling, or whatever you want to call it. I need to stop sleeping with younger guys. They never know what they're doing."

I snort and pick up the folder from my desk, heading to the conference room for an interview with a potential foster family.

It's always such a feeling of accomplishment to have another foster family join us. It's so hard to place kids with the limited families available, so the more the merrier.

My meeting ends up going well, and an hour later they're done with the paperwork and excited for the challenge. They're ready for a placement as soon as we complete their background checks, although that will take a while. Nothing in government moves fast.

I grab a protein bar as I walk by my office to snag the folder I need.

JJ is at her desk, engrossed in a phone call, and doesn't look up when I walk in. She does everything a hundred and ten percent. She'll work her ass off all day and then be ready to go out by this evening.

My next appointment is a site visit. I placed Julio with a new foster family two weeks ago, and today's visit is at their home to see how he's settling in. Julio is eight, and he's about the sweetest kid I've ever met. His dad has never been in the picture, and his mom has been in and out of jail for the past several years, finally relinquishing custody altogether last year.

I've been Julio's case worker since I started at DHS, and I'm completely in love with this little guy. He's been in foster homes since he was four, but none of them seem to stick for more than six months. Some even less.

I hope this one will be a good placement for him.

I take Kelly Drive to the Manayunk house. Even though it's part of Philadelphia proper, the subdivision is so far out of the way that it's almost impossible to get there without driving, especially if you're working on limited time. When I pull into the driveway of the duplex, my heart sinks.

Julio is sitting on the front stoop, staring at the ground.

I climb out of my ancient Toyota Corolla and walk up to him. "Hi, Julio. How is everything going?"

He finally glances up to briefly acknowledge me before looking back down at his feet, but even from that quick glance I could see the sadness in those big brown eyes. "Hi, Miss Holly. It's okay."

"Can I give you a hug today?" I always ask before swooping in.

Some of my kids have bad reactions to any physical touch because of things in their past. Some have just never had any control in their lives and need to have a say in something that happens to them.

Julio nods and stands up. I wrap my arms around him in a quick embrace.

"I missed you, kiddo. How are things with Brad and Linda?"

The older couple has been a foster family for ages. I've placed several kids with them since I started as a case worker, and I've never had any complaints, but Julio doesn't look like he's having the best day.

"They're good. I really like them, but I heard Mrs. Linda say that they're retiring. They don't want to be foster parents anymore. They don't know that I know. Do you think it's something I did?" He looks up at me with such a crestfallen expression that a lump rises in my throat.

"Oh, honey. I'm sure it's nothing you did. Do you want to come inside while I talk with them a while?" I hold out my hand.

Julio takes my hand as we climb the cracked cement front steps. I knock on the door, Julio's hand clinging to mine.

Brad and Linda know the routine after so many years of foster parenting, and the visit goes smoothly. They have the paperwork ready, know what questions I ask, and are ready with answers. After we go through our usual routine, they send Julio upstairs to play in his room.

Linda watches Julio climb the stairs and waits for the bedroom door to close before she turns to me and motions to the living room. We sit down, and she folds her hands in her lap, looking at Brad, and immediately, I know what's coming.

Julio was right.

"Holly, thank you as always for everything you do. It's always a joy to work with you. And you know we've loved being foster parents for so many years."

I nod, waiting. Being a social worker teaches you to be comfortable with silence, to allow people to finish their thoughts rather than jumping in with your own words to fill the space.

"We've made the tough decision that we are going to retire from being foster parents, at least for the time being. Our daughter is pregnant with her first child, our first grandchild, and we want the freedom to go see her and be involved in their lives. We may one day be in a position to take on short-term foster placements again, but for now we need to step back." Linda lets out a relived sigh, like a weight has been lifted, and sits back.

"When will you be retiring? That is, when do you need me to find another placement for Julio?" My voice is calm. I squeeze my hand around my pen, so it doesn't shake. *Please, please give me time to find him a good home.*

Brad and Linda look at each other. Brad clears his throat. "We can take care of Julio through the end of the year."

Shit. The likelihood that I'll be able to find a placement for Julio between Thanksgiving and New Year's is slim. I can't bear to think of him in a group home for the holidays. I realize I'm gripping my pen so hard my knuckles are turning white and force myself to ease up. Foster parenting is a voluntary position, so I can't force them to keep him any longer. I just wish things were easier for him. He's the sweetest kid, and he deserves a wonderful home.

"That sounds fine. Thank you for letting me know. Have you told Julio? Or would you like me to help share the news?"

I hold in my tears until I'm in my car and pulling out of the driveway. Julio was the same stoic little kid I've known for four years. He knew what was coming—he'd overheard them earlier, after all—and he just nodded his head with a sad expression on his face.

I wish, not for the first time, that I could take him home with me. It's a hazard of the job. I became a social worker because I wanted to help kids, but the reality is that you can't always help in the way you want.

The entire thirty-minute drive back to the office, I sit in silence, tears drifting down my cheeks, barely even looking at the Schuykill River. I'll pull it together before I go back into the building, but here in my private space, I let the emotions flow. I cry for Julio. For the kids whose parents don't want them. For the kids who have no parents. For the ones whose parents desperately want them but aren't able to take care of them.

I've been a caseworker for the Department of Human Services since I graduated with my master's in social work. The longer I do this, the more I realize just how blessed I am.

I pull into the lot of the DHS building and find an empty parking space. My phone buzzes with a notification as I pull into the spot.

JJ

Drinks tonight?

. . .

She's insane. So much for the girl who was hungover on our couch a few hours ago. But after this home visit where I got a bomb dropped on me, I need a drink. A big one. One that can make me forget this entire fucked-up situation.

Because I can only ignore Maddox's morning texts for so long. Sooner or later, I'm going to have to talk to him.

4

——————

MADDOX

I send my morning text to Holly, hoping she's willing to talk today. It's been days since The Dinner, as I've been calling it in my head. Every morning I send a *good morning* or a *have a good day* or something else benign. And every day I get crickets. I cross my fingers as I hit *Send*.

HOLLY

Good morning, beautiful.

Good morning

So. My mom and your dad.

Yeah.

You okay with it?

Your mom seems great. It seems
like she makes my dad happy.

But are you okay with it? I know it's
only been a few years since your
mom died.

No, I know. It brings up a lot of
memories and stuff. But she would
have wanted him to move on.

Want to talk? I can call you.

Or dinner tonight?

The three little dots appear, then disappear, then appear again.

HOLLY

I don't think it's a good idea.

Us having dinner? You have to eat.

Us. Dating. With our parents and all.

Fuck. This is what I was afraid of, but I'm smart enough to know that this isn't an argument I'll win over text messages.

> Dinner as friends, then.

The longest two minutes of my life drag by while I wait for the three little dots to turn into words.

HOLLY
Ok.

I strip off my shorts and add them to the hamper. It's too cold out for my body to have produced much sweat during my run, but my five miles did leave me with frozen fingers and toes. As I step into the shower, the steam billows into the bathroom until I close the glass door behind me. The hot water sluices down my body as I start to thaw.

Other than freezing me half to death, my run

didn't do much for me. It certainly didn't do anything to help with the thoughts of Holly that are still burned into my brain.

The heaviness of her breasts under my hands.

The milky softness of her skin.

The way her hips lifted toward me as I bent over her on the couch.

I'm never going to be satisfied with being friends with Holly. Or bring her *brother*. Yeah, our parents are getting married. But we met before that. It's not weird. We're all adults here. I just need to convince her that not only is it okay to pursue this, but that it's meant to be. Because in my mind it absolutely is. I put a hand on the shower wall and lean under the spray, thinking of her.

My cock hardens at the thought of her soft body. I know there's essentially a zero percent chance that I'll convince her to come home with me tonight, so I need to take the edge off before I see her. Make sure I can think with the right head.

I grip my length with one hand, squeezing at the base of my cock and moving slowly to the tip as I stroke myself to the memory of her body. The soft swell of her stomach. The angle of her jaw. Her nipples hardening under my touch. The feel of her heat clenching around me like a goddamn vise. *Fuck.*

I squeeze harder, moving my hand faster as I come, groaning her name.

I pant as the water rinses my cum down the drain. It takes me a full minute before I can stand up straight and wash myself, hoping like hell that it will be enough to help me keep my hands to myself.

Holly needs to come around to this slowly, the idea that dating me is okay even with our parents being together. She's a woman who overthinks things, is beyond cautious. I've known that since the day I met her. It's part of what attracted me to her, if I'm being honest. It's the exact opposite of me in some ways, so it's fucking hot.

I like to analyze things, but once I've thought through the possibilities, I make a decision with confidence. I don't regret, don't rethink things. And I don't give a fuck what most people think.

Yeah, Holly and I are polar opposites when it comes to that.

I don't know what made her push that wariness aside and sleep with me that first night. But I know I've gotten under her skin once before, cracked that armor the tiniest bit.

I just need to do it again.

Salvatore's is right off Rittenhouse, close to the steakhouse where our parents dropped the bomb on us, and it's the kind of place you take a third date. Candlelight, soft music, white table linens, the whole thing. It's not the choice of establishment you take a girl you want to be friends with.

That's the whole point.

Holly looks around as we walk in and I give my name to the hostess. "This seems fancy. This isn't a date, remember?"

Yeah, I remember. And I hate that fact. "I like their lasagna," I say with a shrug, and I'm not lying, either. Their lasagna is the best in the city. It even beats my mom's, but don't tell her that.

The hostess leads us to our table. I do my best to keep my jaw off the ground when Holly slips her arms out of her jacket. A royal blue dress wraps around her gorgeous body, dipping low in the front to reveal cleavage that I'd give anything to bury my face in.

I pull out the chair for Holly, pushing it in as she sits while putting most of my energy into keeping my eyes where they belong. As in, not on her tits, amazing as they may be.

She looks over her shoulder at me and narrows her green eyes in suspicion. "We're having dinner as friends, remember?"

Again, yeah, I remember. Jesus fuck. If she feels the need to remind me of that every thirty seconds, it's going to be a long night.

Instead of backing off, though, I lean over her shoulder to speak low in her ear. "I can still be a gentleman for my friends, can't I?"

She swallows hard. I round the table and take my own seat, smiling innocently at the hostess as she hands us menus.

The conversation flows easily as we order, just like it did over French fries at the diner. I'm struck by how much I like just *being* with Holly. The more time I spend with her, the more I want to be around her. Even if we're not really dating, and there's no chance of anything physical between us tonight. Her company is enough, at least for now.

We split a bottle of red wine that pairs well with my lasagna and her veal parmesan. I love Italian food, and even though it doesn't lend itself to being topped with ketchup, it's typically doused in another tomato-based sauce, which is almost as good.

"How was your week at work?" I ask her as I lift a bite to my mouth. "I'm not sure you told me exactly what you do, actually."

"I'm a social worker."

I chew my bite and swallow. "Like in a hospital?" I

can see her being great at that. Great in any number of social worker jobs, actually. She's easy to talk to. I can see her being a comforting presence during traumatic times. Hell, she's comforting to just be with over dinner.

She shakes her head. "No, I work for the Department of Human Services. Like, foster care."

That might suit her even better, actually. I give a thoughtful nod, swirling a bite of pasta around my plate to pick up extra sauce. "What's your favorite thing about your job?"

She stares at me, that little smile playing at her lips again as she lifts her glass. "I love the kids. Getting to form relationships with them. Seeing them grow. I love the joy on their face when they're reunited with their parents, or when they're adopted. It can be tough, but it's just amazing. Like, I have this one little kid I've known for a few years. His life is rough, and he's been through more than his share of foster homes. But even when life keeps dealing him shitty hands, he still finds a way to be hopeful. He usually gets this big smile across his face when he sees me." As she describes him, a radiant smile builds, but then a frown crosses her face as she describes the kid. It's gone as soon as it appears, and when she falls silent, she's still beaming.

"Your face lights up when you talk about it." It's beautiful, the passion she has for her job and for the kids she helps. I'm curious to know why the frown, what's got her worried or upset, but I know enough about the foster care system that I know there are questions she won't be able to answer.

She blushes. "Yeah. I love it." She pauses with a bite of food halfway toward her mouth, tilting her head. "Thank you. Most people just say, 'that must be tough,' when I tell them what I do. And, I mean, it can be. But there are a lot of good moments, too."

I shrug. "Most people don't want to talk about the worst parts of their jobs. It's not why people choose their careers. We choose our path in life based on what we like."

She nods as she finishes chewing her pasta and darts her tongue out to catch a drop of marinara sauce before she responds. "True. And to answer your earlier question, the week was okay. Nothing that was really a crisis, so that's a bonus. How was your week?" She pauses, thinking. "I don't think you've told me what you do, either."

I take a casual sip of wine. "Nope."

"So... are you going to tell me? Or are you, like, a secret Russian spy and if you tell me, you'll have to kill me?" She lifts her own wine glass, holding it in the air while she looks at me with a small smile.

"Take a guess." This is always a fun game. No one ever guesses right. And I'm enjoying the fact that she's interested in knowing something about me, even if it is just as a friend.

"Do I get something if I guess right?" She's finally relaxed. It would almost border on flirty, if I didn't already know that she's firmly on the side of us not dating. I don't know if it's the conversation or the wine that she's had a glass and a half of. Maybe both.

I lean back in my chair. "Tell you what. I'll make you a bet. If you guess right in three tries, I'll pay for dinner tonight. If you don't, you have to have dinner with me again tomorrow." I lift the wineglass, feeling like a genius for this little spark of inspiration. There's no way she'll get it. No one ever guesses right. It's not a common job by any stretch of the imagination. It's not even a job, really, although my sponsors might disagree.

She mirrors my actions, sitting back with her wine in hand. "Interesting. I'll take that bet." She studies me, her finger running along the lip of her glass as she purses her lips in concentration. "You work in finance."

I shake my head, holding back a smile. "Sort of close. But no."

It's not close at all, in fact. But there are no rules about misleading your competition, and it's not an outright lie.

She taps her chin with her fingers, a smile tugging at her lips, like there's a joke that only she's in on. "Zookeeper."

Huh? Where did that come from? "Um, no. And what in the world would make you think of that?" I feel like I should be offended.

"Your smell."

Yeah, I should be offended. "I don't smell like a—" I break off at the teasing grin that spreads over her face. "Well, joke's on you. That was your second guess. No extra guesses for being mean."

"Aw, did I hurt your feelings?" She takes another sip of her crimson wine.

"Not enough that I won't cash in my winnings. One guess left, Holly. Go ahead and put me in your calendar for dinner tomorrow." I can taste my victory.

"Hmm." She runs her fingers over those lips that I'm dying to kiss again. "Let's see. You're a... poker player."

My mouth falls open. How in the hell did she guess that?

She takes another sip of wine, looking supremely

satisfied with herself, then sets it down and spears a bite of her veal with her fork.

Meanwhile, I'm still just sitting there, unable to form a coherent thought. "Uh… yeah, actually. What the hell made you guess that?"

She slips the veal between her lips and chews, smirking. When she swallows, she picks up her wine glass before she looks me dead in the eyes and says, "Google, *Maddox Anderson.* You showed me your driver's license before I would agree to go home with you. Remember? I texted the picture to JJ and it's still on my phone. So, thanks for dinner."

"Whoa, whoa. It doesn't count if you already knew the answer. That's not fair." I feel myself rapidly losing control over this conversation. Hell, I've already lost control of this entire situation.

"Says who?" she challenges.

"Says… anyone. That's cheating," I stammer. I'm always the one in control. Always. And the way she's so easily wrested it from me in this conversation has thrown me for a loop.

She points at me with her fork. "You should know better than anyone that it's perfectly fair to make a bet when you know exactly what the odds are. Now, where's the waitress? If you're paying, I'm getting dessert."

✳

Holly leans back in her seat and pats her belly. "Oh my God. That was amazing."

I nod, finishing my last bite of tiramisu. "So good."

The waitress places a black folder on the table with my credit card and the check. I open it, write in a tip and the total, then sign it and close the folder. I tuck the card back in my wallet before slipping it back in my pocket.

Holly wipes those luscious lips on a cloth napkin. "Thanks for dinner, Maddox."

I nod as I place my own napkin on the table. "You ready to go?"

She pushes her chair back from the table and slides her coat on. We walk together to the exit. I know we're here as friends. I know she doesn't see us dating. But fuck, this was the best date I've been on in years, even though it wasn't really a date. If she were someone else, I'd be figuring out how to get her back to my place.

As it is, all I have is another date with my right hand this evening.

At the front of the restaurant, we wait together for her ride share. This is a safe area of town, but I know she has an obsession with serial killers and crime. That first night we talked about her love for true crime podcasts and how it results in her being ready to be a victim at any moment, so I figured she'd appreciate someone waiting with her.

It obviously has nothing to do with me wanting to spend every second I can with her.

Holly looks at her phone. "They're almost here. Thank you for dinner, Maddox. It was fun."

Fun is not the descriptor I'd use. Yeah, it was fun. It was also amazing, frustrating, captivating…

I force my brain to focus on the *friend* standing in front of me and try not to scare her off again. "I had a great time, Holly. I always seem to have a great time with you. Thank you for having dinner with me. Can I give you a hug?"

I hold out my arms, and she steps into my embrace just as a black SUV with an Uber sticker in the window pulls up. I brush my lips against Holly's cheek, lingering there to breathe in her scent. She smells warm, like cranberries and vanilla. It's like Christmas morning. When I finally pull back, her pupils are dilated, and her breaths are shallow. She blinks and shakes her head, then sticks her hand out for a handshake.

I smirk as I grip her palm. I'll give her a handshake. Because she can't hide her reaction to me kissing her, even on the cheek. And that means one thing.

That despite her insistence that we shouldn't date, I might still have a chance. I'm not going to let this one pass me by.

5

HOLLY

His beard brushes against my cheek as his lips skim over my cheek. My entire body heats, the scrape of his facial hair jolting right to my core. I thank God that I'm wearing a winter coat, so he can't see my nipples tighten into hard buds.

No. Stop that. No tightening into hard buds or gushing with arousal. This is not a goddamn Harlequin romance. Maddox and I are friends. *Friends.*

My nipples refuse to listen to reason.

"Goodnight, Holly," Maddox says, his voice deeper than usual. He steps back and nods to the ride share that's parked behind us.

I force my voice to function, and finally, one part

of my body is responding to my brain signals. "Um. Goodnight." I turn and check the app to make sure, confirming that the black Jeep is my ride before sliding into the back seat.

As the SUV steers away from the curb and into traffic, I pull out my phone and text JJ.

JJ

> Please tell me you're home.

I can be, what's up?

> Need your help.

Say no more.

I tuck my phone in my purse and lean my head against the cool window beside me, replaying the evening. Maddox had been completely appropriate tonight. I'd asked to be friends, hadn't I? And he'd been nothing but friendly.

So why had I gotten shivers down my spine when he spoke in my ear after he pushed my chair in? And why are my nipples still hard from his goodbye kiss?

It must be the cold. That's why my tits have

decided to go rogue. I cross my arms over my chest and press, trying to force them back to their rightful position, until I catch the driver peeking at me in the rearview mirror.

Forget the nipples. Why am I actually looking forward to seeing him again?

Maddox, I mean. Not the Uber driver, although he's probably a better prospect than my future stepbrother. Pretty much anyone in this city would be a better option.

I shake my head vigorously, trying to shake loose the jumbled thoughts in my mind. It's just because Maddox is the last person I slept with. God, I can't believe I slept with my future stepbrother. At least it's not like I knew it at the time. I just need to go on a date, meet someone new before I have dinner with Maddox again. That's all.

After I won our little bet—okay, I cheated, but who wouldn't?—he decided to go double or nothing. He bet me that I couldn't guess his favorite beer. I figured that was a simple one, since I have a great memory and he ordered an IPA the last time we were at the bar. I figured he was just assuming that I wouldn't remember.

I should have guessed that he was setting me up. He's a professional gambler, after all. I should know that the house always wins. And why didn't I realize that someone's favorite drink was essentially an unprovable thing?

I tried to be cute and guess wrong the first two times, then go in for the kill with my last guess. It worked my way the first time, after all. So I threw out two choices I knew were wrong, then guessed IPA.

I'm still picturing his satisfied smirk when he shook his head. It grates at me a little. Okay, a lot. Especially because I should know that Yuengling is the favorite of every good native Philadelphian. And now I'm on the hook for another two dinners with Maddox.

"JJ?" I call as I slam the apartment door behind me, tossing my purse on the table in the entryway.

I find her in the living room, a bowl of sweet popcorn in her lap. I sink onto the couch next to her and let out a heavy sigh.

JJ holds the bowl out to me. "Kettle corn?"

More food is the last thing I need right now. "I need a date. Maybe more than one. Actually, definitely more than one. I need to get Maddox out of my head. I can't date my stepbrother. It's just—I just can't. Can you help?"

Her grin widens as she sets the bowl of kettle corn down on the coffee table. "I'm glad you're ready. Remember when you told me you needed a date for your dad's wedding?"

I give her a side-eye. "Yes?"

"And remember how I said we'd take care of it?"

Alarm bells sound in my head. "What did you do, JJ?"

JJ holds up her hands in defense. "Nothing, I swear. Nothing yet. I just researched the best dating apps and started a profile for you. It's not live, don't worry."

I open my mouth to protest, but the words catch in my throat. Maybe she has a point. Everyone uses dating apps these days, don't they? Plenty of my friends have met their now-spouses that way, so it's not something that's going to look bad. It could work. Plus, I don't have any other options right now.

I blow out my breath in a resigned sigh. "Okay. But I get to approve everything that goes on that profile. Every. Single. Thing, JJ. And I'm going to need chocolate to get through this."

"What about this one?" JJ holds up her phone.

I wrinkle my nose. "I look terrible in that picture."

We've been going through her photos for half an hour after everything on my phone was deemed unusable as a profile picture. By me, of course. JJ thinks I look fabulous in every picture. Everyone should have a best friend like JJ.

She rolls her eyes. "You do not. How about this?" She scrolls through the photos on her phone and holds it up. It's me at a music festival, the music shell in the background. My dark hair is a wild, wavy mess that's accentuated by the dandelions and violets woven into it.

I shrug. It's not as bad as the first one.

Also, I'm trying to attract a guy who isn't going only for looks, right?

She keeps scrolling. "So we'll use that, and... this one?" She chooses a second photo, this one of the two of us with our arms around each other.

"Aww, I like that one."

JJ grins. "Good. Now we just have to do the profile." She taps on the phone for a few seconds. "How tall are you... five foot three, body type... athletic?"

I snort. "I wish. Put average."

JJ's tongue pokes out the edge of her mouth as she

concentrates. "Single. Interested in men. Now we have to put something about you. How about... 'I'm a social worker with a busy job and the most amazing best friend in the world. I love animals, Italian food, chocolate, and hiking'."

I toss three peanut M&Ms into my mouth and chomp down. "Get rid of the best friend part. And I like hiking, but I haven't gone in years. That seems disingenuous."

"But the best friend thing is true!" She blinks her baby blue eyes at me with a look of pure innocence.

"Give it to me. I'll write something." I snatch the phone from JJ and double check what she's already written. There are only a few words, but I delete them and squint my eyes in concentration as I start to write.

I love my job as a busy social worker. In my free time, I like hanging out with friends, hiking, board games, and...

I pause to think. What else do I like? I swear, every time someone asks me what my hobbies are, I draw a blank. I chew on my lip for a minute, then add *cooking Italian food.*

"There, that should cover it." I hand the phone back to JJ.

She peruses it and nods, then shakes her head. "We need more. Plus, the *cooking* is a stretch. Re-heating pasta doesn't really count as cooking. What are you looking for? What are your turn-ons?"

"Turn-ons? Nothing I would share with a stranger on a dating app." This is sounding more and more like a bad idea.

Do I even need a date for my dad's wedding?

Yes. Definitely, yes. Because there will be family there. The family that saw me at my mom's funeral, being completely humiliated by Jared. I'm sure they already think I'm pathetic. I can't give them more evidence to support that.

I tap my chin in thought. It's time to move on with my life. That's what my dad is doing. I can move on too. "Just say... I'm looking for someone to connect with and enjoy life. That sounds good."

JJ rolls her eyes but taps away on the phone. "Okay. It's done. I'll let you know when your first date is. I don't trust your judgment right now."

My first instinct is to argue, but she's not wrong. Clearly, I choose the wrong guys. For example, Maddox. My future stepbrother. And Jared. A man who has fucked me up in the head so badly I haven't had the will to date in years.

"See if you can make it before Tuesday. I got tricked into having dinner with Maddox again, and I need to go on a date before then."

❄

"Anything?" I look at JJ hopefully from my office desk, where we're both trying to multitask by eating lunch while working on reports.

She turns, looking up from the salad she's eating. "Lots of things. Busy. Why?"

We're both insanely busy this week. I feel bad for even bringing it up, but the clock is ticking. "A date for me? Tonight?"

She spears a tomato with her fork and holds it in the air an inch from her mouth. "Nothing yet. Let me check again." She chews her bite while she picks up her phone and scrolls. "It's looking promising for Thursday. Nothing tonight. Why? You need something to do?"

I pick at my own lunch, tuna salad on wheat bread. "I'm supposed to have dinner with Maddox. Looking for an excuse to get out of it."

JJ spins around in her desk chair and points at me with her fork, a cucumber dangling precariously from the tines. "Do not stand someone up because you found something better. I don't care if you don't like him that way. You're better than that."

I look down at my sandwich, abashed. JJ's moral compass has always pointed straight north, if you don't count sleeping around. She's right. If I stood someone up, she'd never let me hear the end of it. "You're right. I just... it's easier to avoid him."

Because like it or not, my body responds to him. I can't sit across from him at dinner without thinking of how he played my body like an instrument, coaxing climax after climax out of me.

But I can't date my future stepbrother. I can't be an embarrassment to my family the way I was with Jared. I need to find a man that will come to this wedding, say the right things, and maybe not cheat on me at the reception.

The bar is low here.

Maddox is still sending me a text every morning—just a simple *good morning* or *have a good day* or *hope you slept well*. It seems innocent, but I'm sure it's completely calculated to get under my skin. And it has. The worst part is that I've started looking forward to the messages, even though I know I shouldn't.

Not that I'd let him know that, of course. I don't even respond.

JJ swivels back towards her desk and flips a page in the folder she's reading through. "Where are you going for dinner?"

It occurs to me that I don't know. I'm going to

have to text him to find out. I roll my eyes as I type out the message.

MADDOX

Where are we having dinner tonight?

If you need to cancel, that's ok.

I'd never cancel on you. Text me your address. I'll pick you up at 6.

Why?

Because we're going to South Philly, and you don't want to be murdered, do you?

Leave it to Maddox to play into my fears. Maybe I shouldn't have told him just how many true crime podcasts I listen to. I really need to stop watching so much Law and Order, too. It's gotten to the point where I'm just waiting for the day I'm abducted or murdered. Or both. I'm sure that there are plenty of areas of South Philadelphia that are perfectly safe. But he has a point, which is that I would definitely not choose to go there by myself when it's dark out.

I text him the address of our apartment building and turn back to my sandwich, flipping through files. The next folder holds a case file for a child who's newly in the system. I swallow a bite as a lump grows in my throat, the way it always does. Life isn't fair for these kids at all.

"How about this one?" JJ holds up another dress.

I cross my arms, wrinkling my nose. "I don't even think I need a dress. It's not a date."

JJ shrugs, walking out of my bedroom with the two outfits she brought from her closet. I love her willingness to share her clothes, and God knows I'm going to need some good outfits for my upcoming *actual* dates.

But if I'm going to South Philly, I'm wearing jeans. It's freezing out, and no way in hell am I wearing a skirt.

I settle on a pair of bootcut jeans, pairing them with a fitted white top, plaid scarf, and a winter jacket that hides most of the outfit but is definitely necessary with the temperature dropping. I check myself out in the mirror, turning to either side.

Wait. No.

This isn't a date.

I don't care how I look, remember?

If anything, my goal is to make sure he knows we're friends. Nothing more.

I turn away from the mirror and walk through the apartment to the front door. I grab my purse from its usual spot by the door and sling it over my shoulder. The clock on the wall says it's 5:55.

"JJ, I'm leaving!" I call out. I'm hoping to be in the lobby and waiting when he gets there. For some reason, it seems like I'm more in control that way.

"Have fun! Wear a seatbelt and remember, you're both consenting adults and can fuck whoever you want!" she yells back.

Yeah, that's not helpful at all.

I tap my fingers against my hip as the elevator descends. I'm not nervous the way I usually am before dates, which makes sense because, as I keep pointing out, this is *not* a date.

The elevator slows to a halt with a *ding*. As the door slides open, I look out into the small lobby, and my hope of being the one waiting evaporates.

He's standing in the center of the room. Dammit, Maddox.

I stride over to him. "Ready?"

His appraising gaze runs slowly down my body,

and I shiver despite myself. "Ready. Are you okay taking my car? I'm parked right across the street." He brings his eyes to my face. "You look amazing."

"Thanks. I hope I'm dressed okay. You didn't tell me what we were doing or where we were going for dinner." I give him a pointed look, trying to quell the butterflies that flurry in my stomach the moment our eyes met.

He winks. "That's for me to know."

I swear to God, I almost stomp my foot like a toddler. He's so damn infuriating. "I just want to know if I need to change, Maddox."

Maddox turns so he's completely face-to-face with me. He places his hands on my shoulders and looks me square in the eye, the weight of them sending another jolt of electricity though me. "Holly. You look perfect."

I can't pull my gaze away from his dark eyes. There's something so sincere in them that I can't doubt anything he says. My breath hitches slightly.

He reaches out to take my hand. "Are you ready?"

6

MADDOX

When Holly steps off the elevator, I swear my heart skips a beat. She's dressed in casual clothing—jeans, with a puffy jacket—and I've never seen her look more stunning. The casual attire is perfect for what I have planned, although now that I'm looking at her, I want to throw the entire plan out the window and just take her back home and get her naked.

She's starting to stress. I can see it in her expression; her brow pinches together, slightly at first, then more and more until her eyebrows are almost touching. Her mouth tightens, and when she's about to lose it, her nose twitches.

"Are you ready?" I ask, reaching my hand out for hers.

She ignores the gesture, but at least this breaks her stress spiral as we head toward the exit.

I chuckle under my breath. I love this side of her, feisty and standoffish. It's such a contrast to who she is when you get past the wall that she's put up between us.

I catch up to Holly, placing a hand on the small of her back to lead her through the lobby. When we reach the door, I pull it open and motion for her to walk through. "After you."

She sets her mouth in a thin line.

Outside, I pull open the door of the car. It's still warm inside, which is what we need tonight, what with the falling temperatures. I wait for her to buckle her seatbelt before I pull out into traffic.

"So, um, how was your day today?" Holly finally looks at me. "What do you actually do all day?"

Ah, the question everyone wants to ask. When you work anything other than a typical nine-to-five, everyone is intrigued by your schedule.

"It was good. I'm practicing for a tournament this weekend, so that takes up most of my time. My typical day is to wake up, go for a run. I read for a little. Some afternoons I meet with the guys and play poker, like we did today. That typically lasts a few hours. Then we usually go somewhere for a beer, and after that..." I spread my hands as I get to the part of the day we're at now. "If we weren't going out, I might be thinking about playing some online poker, but I usually only do that if there's not a tournament coming up."

Her eyes light with some interest. "What happens in a tournament?"

"This one is in Atlantic City, so it's easy to get to. We'll head there Thursday, stay through the weekend. We just... play poker." I shrug. "It keeps going until everyone loses all their chips except one person."

"So, the group of yours, are they all going?" she asks.

"Only three of us are going this week. Me, Cam, and Blake."

"Do you play as a team?"

I shake my head, holding back a smile. I'll have to teach her how to play poker at some point. "No. It's an individual game. We're just friends. We play together when we can and we like to go to tournaments together because it's fun to road trip and hang out when we're not playing. But when we play, we sometimes play against each other. It's an individual game, and it's every man for himself. We honestly try not to play against one another in tournaments if we can avoid it, because we know one another's tells."

"Your... tells?" Her nose wrinkles adorably.

"Yeah. That's what you call—" I break off as we near our destination, and I maneuver into an open spot on the street. "Hold that thought. Wait here while I grab something. Quick question, though. Pat's or Geno's?"

She looks out the window, excitement dawning when she realizes where we are. We're in South Philadelphia, near the cross streets where the famed cheesesteak rivals sit across from one another. Every good Philadelphian has a preference and will defend it to their dying breath.

Cam, of course, likes Jim's, which is nowhere near the other two, because he has to be special somehow.

"Pat's!" She rubs her stomach. "That sounds so good. Wiz wit'out, please. And fries."

I laugh. "True native right there. Be right back." I step out of the car and close the door, letting her sit in the warmth while I join the line that extends down the block.

Twenty chilly minutes later, I slide back into the car with two cheesesteaks, two cups of fries, and absolutely no feeling in my hands.

Holly's nose wrinkles in confusion when I hand the food to her. "Are we eating in the car?"

I shake my head as I maneuver back out onto the street. "We're going to eat at my place, if that's okay. I was thinking we could maybe play a board game or something."

Holly stares at me, her expression unreadable.

I shrug my shoulder as I make a turn onto Broad Street. "Or not, if that's silly. We could just watch a movie or something."

A smile spreads over her face as she shakes her head. "No. It's not silly at all, Maddox. I love board games. I'm just surprised you do, too."

A laugh escapes. "I play card games for a living. I love all games."

"What's your favorite?" Her eyes shine with excitement.

She's almost hot and cold, but it's more than that. It's like this is the real Holly, and the stressed, shut-off woman is who she wants to show the world. I love these glimpses I get of the real her. I just need to figure out how to convince her that she doesn't need to hide with me.

I purse my lips to the side in concentration. There are so many good games to choose from. "Probably Monopoly. It's a classic. How about you?"

"Ooh, Monopoly is good. I love Ticket to Ride. Code Names. Settlers of Catan. Life. Clue. There are just so many good ones."

We discuss the attributes of different games—required number of players, strategy, time needed to play, attractiveness of the game board. By the time I pull the car to a stop in front of my apartment, we've narrowed it down to two top contenders for tonight: Ticket to Ride and Monopoly. Clue has been wait-listed for a night when we have at least three players.

In the elevator, Holly peers around at the walls and floor. She's avoiding looking at me, a slight blush rising on her cheeks as she bites her lip, and I can practically read all the thoughts written across her face.

Because I'm thinking about it, too.

The last time we were in this elevator. That kiss, the one she initiated. It was one of the sweetest kisses I've ever had. It awakened something in me, something that had me pushing her up against the wall to take more.

I'm getting hard just thinking about it, and I need to do something to make it go down. Think unsexy thoughts.

Baseball. Mom. Parakeets.

"What?" Holly gives me a strange look. "Did you say *parakeet*?"

I try to laugh, but it comes out like I'm choking. "No. Why would I say parakeet?"

She looks like she doesn't believe me, but I don't have a better explanation. Pretty sure nothing shuts down a date—or a non-date—faster than admitting you're thinking about little birds to keep yourself from getting hard.

"Hey!" I let out a burst of mock annoyance.

Holly giggles as she records her points. "Aw, did you need that route?"

I did, and she knows it. That's the only reason she claimed the route that was nowhere near her other train cars.

Like with most board games, there are two types of people who play Ticket to Ride: the ones who focus on their own game and occasionally play defense when someone inadvertently blocks them, and the ones who win by sabotaging other players.

I think I just learned what type of player Holly is. Too bad for her, though; I can beat her at her own game. She thinks she's on some kind of moral high ground right now because I put ketchup on not only the French fries, but also on my cheesesteak. For the record, it's provolone wit'—in other words, provolone cheese with peppers and onions on the cheesesteak—and wit' ketchup. You will never convince me otherwise.

I line up six train cars and set them on the long route between Houston and El Paso. "Fifteen points." And another route completed, even with her little attempt at sabotage.

She picks up two cards. "Tell me more about your tournament this weekend. You said it starts Thursday, right?"

I nod as I draw my cards. "Yep. We'll drive over there Thursday morning."

"Bummer. Guess you'll have to wait till next week to have another dinner with me."

I watch as she lays down another short route. "Guess so, unless you want to come to Atlantic City. Could be a fun road trip."

"Nah. I have to work." She studies her cards. "Plus, I have plans on Thursday."

I take a sip of lager out of the glass bottle in front of me while she contemplates her move. "Going out with JJ?"

One side of her lips turns up in a smirk. "I have a date."

Sometimes it comes in really, really handy to have a

good poker face. When you're playing poker, obviously. Also, when you're about to trounce someone in a board game without them ever seeing it coming. But right now, I'm glad my face doesn't show what I'm thinking, because what I'm thinking is, *I want to kill the guy she's going out with.*

Instead, I say, "A date, huh? That's interesting. Where did you meet him?"

She fiddles with her cards. Unlike mine, her poker face is abysmal. "A dating site."

"Hmm." I draw cards for my turn.

"What does that mean?"

I look up from my cards, my face still a mask of calm. "It doesn't mean anything."

She sets the cards down and crosses her arms over her chest, drawing my attention to the cleavage I want to bury my face in. Yeah, I'm looking there. I'm not a saint. And she may think it's not a good idea for us to date, but I have other plans.

"Don't judge me for going on a dating site. I need a date for the wedding. And besides, I'm twenty-eight. I'm ready to meet my soulmate."

I reluctantly pull my gaze away from her tits and place my own cards face-down as I lean back. "And you think this date could be your soulmate?"

"He could be." She shrugs and blinks with those

long lashes. "If not, I'll go on another date."

"So, you're planning to meet your soulmate in time for the wedding. In less than six weeks."

"You never know. Maybe I won't know if he's my soulmate. I just want to meet the right guy. And you can fall in love in six weeks. People do it all the time," she shoots back.

My eyebrow quirks upward. "Your date for the wedding will be someone you're in love with."

"That's my plan." She picks up her cards again and examines them, tapping her fingers on the backs in a rat-a-tat that would seem benign, but when I look at her face, she's biting her lip.

I haven't known her that long, but I can already tell she's stressed and overwhelmed thinking about this. Why is she so fixated on having a date for the wedding, and so against dating me?

She lays down three cards to claim a route.

I don't touch my cards. For some reason I don't yet understand, I want to make her feel better. I want to see that carefree laugh. "Let's make a bet."

She rolls her eyes. "I'm not adding more dinners to the one I already owe you, Maddox. I'm busy meeting my soulmate."

I shake my head and wait until she meets my gaze before I pull the corners of my lips up in a smile. "You still owe me one after today, but no, that's not the bet. You think you can find love in six weeks, right? Here's the deal. If you bring a man to that wedding that you're in love with, like *really* in love with, I'll pay up. Twenty grand."

She lets out a little puff of air. "Yeah, right."

"Fifty."

Her face scrunches up in confusion. "You'd pay me fifty thousand dollars?"

I threw out the idea without really thinking it over, but now I'm into this. "Yep," I say, popping the *p*. "You come to that wedding with a guy that you're in love with, who loves you back, fifty grand is yours, no questions asked."

She holds up a hand, her eyebrows knitted together. "I have questions. Like... why?"

I shrug. Mostly, it's to do something to take her mind off of things. And honestly, I have enough money that this isn't a huge amount to me. Listening to her talk about her work, her passion for the kids she helps, I know she'd use the money wisely.

Those fingers are drumming on the table now. "And second, what do you want if I lose? Not that I'm going to. But just in case."

I hadn't thought that far, but I'll take the opening. "You. You lose the bet, you agree to date me. Not as friends, not a one-night stand. But actually give us a shot."

We shake hands to seal the bet.

The stakes we agree on are this: Holly has until our parents' Christmas Eve wedding to fall in love. She has to swear she's in love, and the guy she brings to the wedding has to say he loves her back. That's it. I'll deposit the money in her bank account by New Year's. If she loses, she'll give up on the lame excuse that our parents like one another and agree to give us a chance to have a real relationship.

I'm learning from our game night that Holly is intensely competitive. Even more competitive than me, maybe, which is saying something. I'm sure Holly has no intention of losing this bet. But I never make a bet without a very clear understanding of the risk involved and without weighing things carefully.

I may have made this bet for fun, but now I'm invested. I'm not going to lose this one.

We're packing up the pieces of Ticket to Ride when both of our phones vibrate at the same time. For the record, she won the game. This time. But it was close.

Holly picks up her phone first and looks at the message, her expression unreadable. "I think you got the same message I did."

I check my phone.

MOM, ADDIE, JOSIE, AND HOLLY

Hi kids, it's Mom.

And hi Holly, it's Judy.

Robert and I would like to invite all of you to my *house emoji* for Thanksgiving *turkey emoji*

We will have *wine emoji* *beer emoji* *cake emoji* let me know if you want to bring something, but we'd just *heart emoji* to have you there!

Jesus, it's like reading a fucking Highlights magazine. You know, the ones for little kids who can't read, so they put little pictures for the hard words. That's what happens when your little sister teaches your mom about emojis.

MOM, ADDIE, JOSIE, AND HOLLY

Holly: Thanks, Judy. I'll be there.

Maddox: I'll be there. Stop using emojis, Mom.

Mom: *heart emoji* you all.

Holly's text pops up just as I hit *Send* with my last text. She looks over at me when she reads my reply. I can tell from her face that she wasn't expecting me to accept.

"You're going, too?" she asks, then shakes her head. "I mean, of course you're going. It's your mom's house. I don't have to go."

I put the phone down and fold the game board into the box. "Of course I'm going. It's Thanksgiving. Mom's turkey is amazing. You should come."

She chews her lip. "I don't want it to be weird."

I take two steps, closing the distance between us. I place two fingers under her chin to tilt it up so she has to meet my eyes. "It's not weird. I enjoy being around you." I run my thumb over her lower lip, the one I want to nibble on.

Her cheeks flush, and her pupils dilate as I bring my lips to her ear. "I can behave myself if I have to. Can you?"

7

HOLLY

J J forwards me the information for my date on Thursday afternoon, three hours before the date itself—enough time to prepare, not enough time to stress out so much that I lose my nerve.

My first contender for Mr. Right is named Charles. He's thirty, loves Italian food, and works as an accountant. His profile picture is of a man wearing a baseball cap, the Phillies stadium behind him. I mentally add baseball to his list of likes. He looks cute, at least from the picture.

I'm meeting him at Table 12, a trendy BYO restaurant in Center City. I arrive before he does and check my watch. It's 6:58, so I'm actually early, although it would have been a point in his favor if he'd gotten here before me.

The hostess shows me to a table. I hand her the bottle of Malbec I picked up on the way here. The BYO—bring your own—restaurants don't sell alcohol, but you can bring it in, and they'll serve it for you.

At 7:05, I'm still waiting, and I let the waitress pour me a glass.

This is fine. Maybe he got held up with a work emergency. Accountants have emergencies at work sometimes, don't they?

I mean, probably not the same kind of emergencies doctors would have to deal with. And probably not even the same kind of emergencies we have at the office when we need to urgently take custody of a child to get them out of an unsafe situation. But I'm sure there's some kind of accounting emergency that could come up. Probably.

I take a sip of my wine, then a second sip. Today was stressful at work, even more than usual. I'm still searching for a placement for Julio for after the holidays. I've called my usual contacts, but no one can take him. It's understandable that no one would be prepared to take on a new foster kid so close to the holidays, and I know a lot of the social workers in my department would just accept that he'll need to be in a group home for a few weeks. But I think of that precious boy in what is, essentially, an orphanage, just prettied up with a nicer name. I can't give up on him like that.

I take another sip of wine, nodding to myself. I'll find a place for Julio. Maybe an emergency placement would work. We had to find one of those today for a baby, and just as much as thinking of Julio, maybe even more so, this one wrecked me. The baby was left in one of the Baby Safe Haven boxes by the fire station.

I blink back a tear as I imagine him being left there. Did he know what was happening? Was he confused when his mother put him there and never came back, leaving him with strangers?

The boxes are such a good thing, they really are. Almost every state has laws allowing you to surrender your baby, no questions asked, but the boxes are becoming more common, too. They're a safe place, warm and dry, and as soon as a baby is put in there an alarm goes off, so a baby is never in there for more than a minute or two by themself.

It's saved so many unwanted babies. But just the idea that someone wouldn't want such a precious thing always gets to me. This little one is safe now, happy with one of my favorite foster families.

I mentally cross my fingers that they'll be able to keep this little one for a while.

I bring the wine glass to my lips and sip again. I

check my watch. 7:09. This is not a good impression for a first date, buddy.

"Holly?"

I turn at the voice to find a man who vaguely resembles the photo I saw of Charles. He's taller than me, although not by much. He's bald, now that he's not wearing his baseball cap.

I smile and nod. "Yes. You must be Charles. It's nice to meet you."

He shakes my hand before sliding into the seat opposite me. "Chip, actually. I've heard good things about this place, but I've never eaten here before. What about you?"

No mention of your tardiness, huh, *Chip*?

I force a smile. "No, this is my first time here. I was thinking about getting the veal."

He wrinkles his nose and looks at the menu.

Oooo-kay.

It's not a bad date. I mean, it could be much worse. But it's just... not good. Not like when I had dinner with Maddox, even though that was just as friends.

The conversation with Chip doesn't flow. I don't wonder what it would be like to kiss him. The thought doesn't even cross my mind. I don't get butterflies in my stomach, wondering whether he'll ask for a second date, because I already know there won't be one. I pick at the last few bites of veal on my plate.

"Would you like to see a dessert menu?" The waitress pauses at our table, picking up Chip's empty plate.

I put my fork down on my plate and slide it toward her. "No, thanks. Just the check." I'm ready for this night to be over. I just want to relax with JJ and start looking for the next prospect for Mr. Right.

Chip doesn't argue, and when the check arrives, he doesn't argue over that either. He lets me reach for it, then slides his card in, too.

I'm a modern woman. I don't need men to buy me dinner. Just... the gesture is nice. That's all.

It's fucking freezing out here.

Chip offers his hand again, shivering in the icy wind. "I had a nice time tonight."

Did you, now, Chip?

I shake his hand, grateful he didn't go in for a kiss that I'd have dodged. "Thanks, Chip. It was nice meeting you."

"Have a good night, Holly." He gives me a wave

and turns to walk down the sidewalk, pulling his coat up to his ears.

I only have to wait a few minutes for my rideshare to pull up. It's a safe area, and I'm in front of a well-lit restaurant, so it's pretty unlikely that I'll end up as a victim on a true crime podcast, but it's still freezing, and it's the nice thing to do.

Maddox would have waited with you. He would have offered you his coat.

I push those thoughts to the back of my brain, rationalizing. Of course Maddox would have waited. He's my friend. That's what friends do. Charles—Chip—was just a date, a bad one at that, and I'm not going to see him again. He doesn't owe me anything.

So, it's fine that I'm waiting here alone, trying to shield myself from the wind.

Unbidden, my thoughts turn back to the baby we took into custody today. He was all alone. Tears prick my eyes. I don't get emotional over my cases usually, but this one tore at my heart.

I wish I had someone I could tell about the little guy. Jack. That's what we called him, since he didn't have a name. JJ would understand, but she's a master at separating personal from professional.

My phone buzzes to alert me that my ride is here. I look down at the screen to swipe away the notification.

There's a text from Maddox waiting, too.

MADDOX

How's your date?

I climb into the waiting sedan after checking the license plate against the information in the app and type out a reply.

It was fine.

Ouch. That bad, huh?

Let's just say he wasn't my soulmate.

Well, I'm not going to say I told you so.

You just did.

wink emoji

How was the rest of your day?

Tough. Long day, long story.

> Want to talk? I'm between games.
> Can I call you?

I chew on one side of my lower lips as I consider. He's a good listener. I know that much. And we're friends, after all.

> Ok. I'm in an Uber, and I'll be home in a few. I'll call you then.

My finger hovers over the phone screen.

I lie on my bed, staring up at Maddox's contact information on the little lighted screen.

I've been home for ten minutes and I haven't called him. What would I even say to him? How much of today's crap can I dump on him?

I'm not sure we're the kind of friends who spill about bad days and how work is getting under our skin. Maybe he just wants to say hi, hear a funny story about how the date went. Maybe he's just being nice.

I reach over to put my phone on the nightstand and almost drop it when it starts buzzing insistently.

FaceTime call from Maddox.

I am *so* not ready for a video call, but on the plus side, my makeup still looks reasonably good from the date. I swipe to answer, and his gorgeous face comes into view.

"Hey. Everything okay?"

His voice is so full of concern that I burst into tears, letting out everything that I've been holding back all day.

"Oh, baby, I'm sorry. Let it out." He waits patiently, silent while I sniffle and sob and even blow my nose into a tissue while he watches.

God, I'm glad we're not dating. I'd be mortified to do that in front of a guy I was seeing. But we're just friends, so it's okay.

When I finally draw in a shaky breath and swipe the mascara that's started to run—so much for nice makeup—he smiles. "There you go. Tell me what's going on."

I swallow against the lump in my throat that's been there most of the day. "It's just work. It's nothing. I'm sorry to unload on you like this. It's nothing you can fix, anyway."

His brows knit together. "Holly, it's not nothing. It's something that's important to you, so it's important to me."

Even through the small screen of my phone, I can see the sincerity in his eyes.

I breathe in and lift my shoulders, then exhale as I drop them. "It's a case at work. A baby safe haven. It's just... hitting me hard, I guess. The idea that someone could just give up a baby. I know, logically, that the baby is probably better off with a family that wants it and can provide for it, but..." I search for the right words. "Just the idea that no one wants him. He didn't do anything wrong or do anything to cause this. He's so innocent."

I wipe away another tear and wait. For the optimism, the reassurance that I've done everything I can, that the baby is better off. Any number of platitudes that people employ in these scenarios.

Maddox is silent, though. For a second, I think the call is frozen because he's so still, but then he tilts his head. "I'm so sorry, Holly. That's really sad. It must be hard for you to see that."

And just like that, I tear up again. No rationalizing. No false optimism. No attempt to comfort the crying woman, to get her to pack away her tears. There's not even pity in his voice.

Simply unwavering support. Acknowledgement of my feelings. Understanding.

I wipe away yet another stray tear. "Dammit,

Maddox. How do you always know the right thing to say?"

He finally grins, one side of his lips pulling up. "Years of practice. And... two sisters."

A laugh bubbles up, getting mixed up with the remnants of a sob.

His eyes crinkle with a smile. "So. How was the date for real?"

I feel lighter, somehow, after talking to Maddox. It's refreshing. I've never been one to have male friends, or lots of friends in general. I find my person or people and stick with them through thick and thin, and JJ— my ride or die—is more of a fixer. She wants to offer solutions, not just listen.

The guys I've dated in the past were never ones for conversation like this, either. So maybe it's less of a guy thing and more just a Maddox thing.

I can't believe I cried on the phone with him. It must be getting close to my period. I go through this emotional roller coaster about once a month. And it usually coincides with me being hornier than usual.

I squeeze my thighs together. Yep, definitely that time of the month. That's got to be the explanation for all of this. The hormones have to be responsible for my tears and the fact that I want to go over to Maddox's apartment and jump his bones right now.

But we're friends. We don't fuck anymore.

When I'm in this mood, it's impossible to sleep unless I get some, shall we say, relief. I put my phone on the nightstand face-down, so the FBI can't see what I'm about to do, on the off chance that they really do spy on everyone through our phone cameras. You never know.

I pull open the top drawer of my nightstand and root until my hand closes on silicone.

My trusty rabbit vibrator. The hot pink one that JJ made me buy the time she dragged me to a sex toy party back in grad school. I told her I would never forgive her for embarrassing me like that. Until I tried it.

I mean, I'm still never going to forgive her for mortifying me like that. But this little rabbit didn't turn out to be such a bad purchase after all.

I send an exploratory hand between my legs. Yep, no need for lube. I slide the vibrator inside me slowly, turning on both the twisting and vibrating functions.

My eyes roll back in my head. Oh God. I arch as the sensations start to spread over me, the rabbit bringing a quick and reliable orgasm, faster than any guy out there.

Another climax builds right on the tails of the first one. And it has nothing to do with Maddox. It's not his dick that I'm imagining inside me, thrusting so deep that I have to bite my lip to keep from moaning out loud. It's not his voice I'm hearing in my mind. And it's definitely not his face I'm picturing as I come, over and over and over.

Not. At. All.

8

MADDOX

"Call." I toss chips into the pile, matching the current bet.

My adrenaline pulses through me the way it always does at a big tournament. I sit on the edge of my seat, never letting myself get too comfortable. I'm looking at a pair of eights. Not the best pair of hole cards, but as I study the other players' faces, it's clear that no one else has anything going for them either.

One by one, players fold as we make our way around the table until there are only three of us left. The dealer lays out the three cards of the flop: queen, ace, nine, all different suits.

I still have nothing, but neither do any of these

guys. I can tell by their expressions, but more importantly, the cards don't lie. I know the odds.

The man next to me checks, staying in without putting any money in the pot. I raise. Time to see who's going to call my bluff.

Player number three folds like a pansy.

Player one calls my bet, and the dealer puts down the turn. A queen. I'm looking at two pair. I watch the other player carefully.

He checks again, confirming my theory. He's got nothing.

I look at my cards, at the community cards laid out on the table, then back at player one, like I'm contemplating a big decision, even though I've had this plan since before the hole cards were dealt.

I push a large pile of chips into the center. "Raise."

Player one glances at his cards one more time, like they're going to show him something new, before he tosses them face-down on the table with a grunt. "Fold."

I keep my expression neutral while I sweep the chips toward me, winning the hand without having to show my cards.

Statistically, one of the other players would have had a better hand than I did. Probably more than one.

But that doesn't matter. All that matters is what

they think I had. That's the beauty of poker. All that matters is what people believe.

Pushing the bet like this is my favorite tactic. Nudge people into folding their hands by raising the bet, even when I'm bluffing. Which I am most of the time. Eventually, they'll start to catch on that maybe I'm bluffing, because no one can have that many good hands in a row.

Then, when they try to call my bluff, I go all in on a good hand.

It's about the long game. It's not one hand, one card.

Just like it's not about one night or one date with Holly. I hate the idea that she's going on dates with other men. We're so right for one another, and I wish she could see it the same way, but I'll wait as long as I have to. It's torture hearing about her dating other guys. But I like Holly. I enjoy talking to her, spending time with her, so I'll take whatever I can get for now and work toward building her trust in me.

But that doesn't mean I have to be happy with her going out with other guys, or truly commiserate with her over bad dates. I had to hide my gleeful smile last night when she told me how miserable her date was.

One hand down and more chips in my corner.

There was no hiding the gleeful smile when my

phone rang again. It only took a minute to realize Holly hadn't meant to call me. The soft buzzing noises confused me at first, until I heard her moan. It was muffled, but I thought I heard her say my name. I'd put myself on mute and let her finish before I ended the call and went to take care of myself.

A new set of cards is dealt out. I have a ten and a queen, both clubs. I take in the piles of chips in front of the other players. Most are dwindling, so their risk perception is going to be skewed. Most players won't bet big on the pre-flop, when we bet just based on the two cards in our hands, before we see any of the community cards.

I do, tossing in a pile of chips. One by one, the other players fold, unwilling to take their chances, and I rake in my chips and a little bit extra.

As the dealer passes out cards for the next hand, two of the other players are watching me intently. I hide my smile, not even letting my lips twitch. Here it is. They're getting ready to call my bluff. I'll either need to fold this hand or have something good.

God, I love this game.

I look at the cards in my hand. Two kings. Close to a seventy percent chance of winning against almost anything but pocket aces. This time, when I raise, the two players who were studying me at the deal match my raise.

The flop has a queen, a king, and a ten.

The turn card is the king of diamonds.

The river gives us a jack. There's a chance someone has a straight, but the suits in the community cards are off, so it won't be a straight flush, the only thing that could beat my four kings.

"All in." I push all of my chips to the center.

The two remaining players do the same.

We lay down our hole cards over to show the table, and like I already knew, they don't have anything. Two pairs each. Not good enough to beat my four of a kind.

The two men each give me a nod as they rise to leave the table, out of chips and out of the tournament. I offer them a smile, the first one I've let cross my face since I sat down at the table.

Cam hands me a Jameson on the rocks. It's exactly what I need after a full day of poker. As much as I love the game, tournaments can be draining. Practice sessions only last an hour or two and don't really take the focus of a real tournament, and online gaming only lasts until I decide to log off. Tournaments, on the other hand, last all day, and you have to be on for every second of them.

I take a long sip, appreciating the burn as the liquor flows down my throat.

"Nice game today." Blake nods over his own glass.

"Thanks," I say, raising my drink. I made something in the neighborhood of a hundred grand today by being the ultimate winner of the tournament. I suppose I should put some of it in a separate account, on the off-chance Holly finds someone to fall in love with and I have to pay up.

But the thought makes my stomach twist.

Not the money. I don't give a shit about that. But the idea that she could actually fall in love with someone else.

I don't make bets without weighing the odds and likely outcomes, but this one I threw out without really thinking, which is way out of character for me. I'm starting to wonder if this was a good bet after all.

When it comes to Holly, suddenly I'm doing lots of things that are out of character for me.

When we FaceTimed last night, she was so vulnerable, honest. My heart broke for the baby that was surrendered. I can't imagine what it's like to see the seedy underbelly of society, day in and day out. To take care of children who are neglected, abandoned, or even those who are desperately wanted but whose parents can't take care of them.

It's clear just how much of herself Holly pours into her job. It was a side of her I hadn't seen before, and fuck, I might have already fallen a little bit in love with her.

I take another sip of my whiskey. I need to clear my head, figure out my next move. The tournament will start up again tomorrow evening, but it's three in the morning, and I doubt she's awake. I send a text, both to cover my morning text and to see if she's up.

HOLLY

> Good morning, beautiful. It's been a long night of poker, but I just wanted to let you know I'm thinking of you. Looking forward to seeing you in a few days. Dinner Tuesday?

"Texting your girl?" Cam lifts his glass of cola as a smile plays at his lips.

I scowl, jamming the phone back in my pocket. "None of your business. When you assholes find the one, you'll be distracted, too."

Blake chuckles. "Yeah, that'll be the day."

Cam clinks glasses with him. Ellie must have broken up with Cam again. We'll see how long that lasts this time.

I don't know what it is about Ellie. To me, she seems like a calculating bitch, but maybe I'm projecting my own past relationship onto her. I honestly don't know why he keeps going back to her, other than some deep-rooted fear of failure. Like if he gets back together with her, maybe it'll work this go round and they can ignore the fact that they've broken up twenty times.

We spend a while sipping our drinks. The danger of casinos is that they give you free alcohol as long as you're playing, so you have to pace yourself. And even more dangerous are the railbirds, the girls who hang out at casinos just hoping for a chance with the poker players.

On a weekend like this, they swarm to us like moths to a light.

None of the guys I hang out with have ever really been into the scene of casino girls and railbirds, thank goodness. They're a recipe for disaster.

I take a sip of my whiskey and let out a sigh.

"What's wrong?" Blake clinks the ice in his glass as

he frowns at me. "Don't tell me you're replaying your hands in your head. You had a great day."

I shake my head. "Nah. It's the girl. She wants to be friends. I'm playing the long game here. I just wonder if it's going to pay off."

Cam tips back the last of his soda. "Is she worth it?"

I sit upright, looking him dead in the eye. "Yeah, man. One hundred percent."

He meets my gaze. "Then you have to believe it's going to pay off. Don't give up."

A deep thought from a guy who breaks up with his girl every couple of weeks, but maybe he's on to something.

I nod, deep in thought. "I'm going to head to bed. I want to get some sleep and be up in time to talk to Holly before we start up again tomorrow." I down the last of my drink and place the glass on the table with a heavy thud.

Blake and Cam exchange glances.

I'm not in the mood for their judgment. I just want to get back to my room, take off my pants, and jerk off while I picture Holly's body.

"You sure you're in a good spot with all of this?" Cam finally breaks the silence.

Cam and Blake are as close to me as brothers. We've been supporting one another through tournament wins and losses, girlfriends that have come and gone. We're family. But we've always prioritized one another over girls.

Until now.

"I'm back in town. You still up for dinner this week?" I ask as soon as Holly answers her phone.

No time for pleasantries. I hold the phone between my shoulder and my jaw as I dump a load of clean laundry onto my bed from the laundry basket.

We got back to town yesterday after a very long weekend that ended up being fairly lucrative for all three of us. My sponsors will be happy with my performance. Honestly, though, I'm surprised I was able to focus at all. My mind is so absorbed with Holly these days.

Holly sounds like she's somewhere downtown, the sounds of traffic audible in the background.

"Sure, if we can find a time. I'm busy tomorrow. Wednesday is Thanksgiving eve, so I'm going out with JJ. Then Thanksgiving at your mom's house."

"Whatcha doing tomorrow?" I try for a casual tone. It sounds like I'm slurring my words, and I cringe. Jesus, it's five in the evening, and I'm not even drinking.

"Um, I have a date," she says softly.

Of course she does. She doesn't sound excited about this one, but who would after the disaster she described from her last date?

"Another online dating find?" I sort through the clean clothes. I should hire someone to do this, but I have a very precise way I like to fold things, and none of the housekeepers I've hired in the past have ever gotten it exactly right.

"Yeah. His name is Justin."

I fold a pair of socks together, then look closer and realize they don't match. I unfold them and toss both back on the pile. "Interesting."

Holly laughs, the sound going right to my balls. "Yeah. He seems like a nice guy. I'll let you know how it goes."

Sure, she will. Is it wrong for me to hope the guy is another limp dick like the one she went out with last week?

I realize I'm gripping the washcloth I'm folding so hard my knuckles are white and force myself to relax. "Sounds good! Have fun." It does not sound good. I do not want her to have fun. "Are you planning to take the train to Ardmore on Thursday?"

"Yeah, I am. Want to coordinate so we can ride together? I was thinking of bringing a pie, but on public transport..." She trails off, and I can picture her hands out, palms up. "Anyway, I decided I'm just going to bring wine. That seems safest."

I stare at a shirt as she hangs up. Why does it look all wrong? It takes me a minute before I realize it's inside out. By the time I get it turned correctly, I've lost motivation to fold it, but I force myself to do my best.

Because I can do laundry. Because I'm a catch.

I just need her to figure that out before I completely fall apart.

HOLLY

Train leaves 30th Street at 10:45 or 12:45. Think we should be there at 11:05 or 1:05?

What time is dinner?

I'll text Mom.

MOM

Hi Mom- what time for dinner Thursday? Or what time should I be there?

Dinner's at 4. Come anytime. Josie and Chris get here Wednesday morning.

HOLLY

Dinner's at 4. My sister and her wife will be there Wednesday night, so I feel like I should get there earlier in the day to provide a buffer. Is 10:45 okay with you?

Sure. I'll see you then.

What's your sister's name? I've met Addison, but you said there's another one?

Josie. She's quiet, kind of a tough nut to crack, but I think you'll like her.

CAM

Thanksgiving with the family?

Yeah, headed to my mom's place in Ardmore. You?

No real plans. *shrug emoji*

Want to join us? It's going to be a shitshow with my mom's new fiancé, Holly, and my sisters. I could use backup.

You sure?

Of course, man, you're family. Just don't fuck my baby sister.

eyeroll emoji

MOM

One more for dinner, Mom. Cam is coming, if that's okay.

Of course! He's more than welcome. The more the merrier.

Unless he's doing some weird vegan thing like Addie did that one year. I'm not making Tofurkey again.

9

HOLLY

It's just a date.

I breathe out, staring myself down in the mirror. I can do this.

JJ set up this dinner with a guy named Justin. This one's profile says he's 35, a surgical tech who works at one of the local hospitals. He has hair—I double checked—and it's light brown. I can't tell from the photo what color his eyes are, but they're light. There are no obvious red flags in his profile.

We're meeting at a new bar-slash-bowling alley in Center City. It's supposed be super fun. I'm actually excited for this one. At the very least, it should be enjoyable, even if the guy is a dud.

I take a few steps back to check out my outfit. JJ more or less dressed me, offering up one clothing option after another of hers until I found something that I liked and she approved of.

It took two hours.

The Uber drops me off in front of 10Pinn, the trendy bowling alley where I'm meeting the gentleman du jour. I climb out of the car and adjust my shirt and hair, hoping to look presentable before I go in to try to find him.

"Holly?"

I startle, almost tossing my purse in the air, but I recover quickly. Justin is waiting on the sidewalk for me.

"I thought we could meet out here and head in together. Less awkward, you know?" He laughs.

As I recover from the initial shock of finding him here instead of inside, I realize it's actually a really sweet gesture. "Sure, that sounds good. No sitting alone at a table waiting for someone not to show up, right?"

Wait. That makes me sound like I've been stood up in the past. Abort. Abort.

I backtrack. "I mean, it's just much nicer to go in as a couple." Wait, are we a couple? That sounds like I think we're a couple. Hold on.

Before I can backpedal and embarrass myself, Justin offers his arm, and I grasp it through his coat.

Even through the layer of fleece, I can tell he's solid. I appreciate his offer to walk in together, too. It *is* awkward and uncomfortable to walk into a place alone, trying to see if a face matches the one you think you're meeting. There's the sense that everyone else can tell you're there on either a blind date or a first date with someone you met through a dating app, and they're all silently judging you.

It turns out Justin actually had the foresight to reserve us a lane. This turns out to be key; the place is insanely busy for a Tuesday night. The bowling balls are stacked behind the sitting area at each lane, and we peruse the selection. I look for the lightest option, settling on a pale blue one that weighs eight pounds, while Justin chooses a twelve-pound red-and-black ball.

I watch the muscles in his forearm ripple as he lifts his ball and places it on the ball return next to mine.

Justin touches my lower back lightly. "I'll go get us some drinks while you set up the game board. What can I get you to drink?"

I request a vodka cranberry. He heads to the bar, and I turn to the screen to enter our names. This date is already going better than the last one. He's refreshingly normal, considerate, and reasonably good-looking. Not as good-looking as Maddox, but definitely a safer option.

"STRIKE!" I do a little dance, shimmying my butt as I walk back to the seats.

Justin wraps his arms around me in a congratulatory hug, and I look up at him, smiling.

He really does have a nice face. JJ picked out a good one this time. Good on paper, nice in person.

Justin dips his head to give me a peck on the lips. Just a peck. He unwraps himself and steps back. "I really like hanging out with you, Holly."

"Same," I answer honestly. And I do. I like the thought of seeing him again. There might not be butterflies, but those will come with time. I think.

Justin pays for our date. He's polite, respectful, sweet. *Check, check, check.* He puts a hand lightly on the small of my back as we walk to the exit. Outside, he waits with me for my ride share and offers me his coat, which I politely decline.

I check my phone, ignoring a handful of text messages to see where my ride is. About four minutes away. I share this information with Justin.

"Thanks for waiting with me. I'm probably not

going to get abducted here, but I don't want my story to end up as an SVU episode." I smile at him.

"Hey, I get it. I love that show, but it gives you ideas."

I laugh, nodding. He gets it.

Justin takes a step closer to me. "Can I see you again?"

"I'd like that," I say.

His perfect white teeth are on display as he smiles. None of those smile lines around his eyes, but no one's perfect, right? "Is it too much to hope you're free tomorrow night?"

I chew on the inside of my cheek. I'm just going out with JJ, but she'd kill me if I canceled plans with her for a guy. "I have plans tomorrow, actually. I'm going to a bar with my best friend. She's cool, though. If you want to join us, that would be great, or maybe we can try for next week."

"I'd love to meet her if she's cool with me crashing your girls' night. What bar?"

"Darby's," I whisper as he steps a little too close. He's good-looking. We get along, and we had a good date. We're talking about another one, for Christ's sake. It's not supposed to feel weird.

Justin tucks a stray lock of hair behind my ear. "Can I kiss you, Holly?"

I nod, because what else does one do here? I can't ruin my chances with this one. His lips come down on mine, and it's like the peck on the lips he gave me earlier. It's sweet, respectful. It feels... okay. I can work with this, I think.

He breaks away and steps back as a car pulls up. "I had a really nice time tonight, Holly. I'll text you." He looks over my shoulder at the car. "Check the license plate against the app."

MADDOX

How's the date going?

Must be good. Can't wait to hear about it, babe.

JJ

How's the date going? Is he as hot as his picture?

You better give me details, bitch.

JUDY

eyeballs emoji forward to seeing you Thursday, dear! Let me or your dad know what time your *train emoji* gets in and we'll pick you up.

DAD

train time

what

what time is

call me train

I snort at the last one. Dad has never really figured out texting. I think he gets flustered by how small the touchscreen keyboard is on his phone. He usually types out a few words and then gives up, or inadvertently hits *Send* before he means to.

I call him first. "Hi, Dad. Did you want to know what time the train gets in on Thursday?"

"Yeah. Judy said we should pick you up. I think her son is coming in from the city, too. Maybe you can coordinate so we only have to come out once. I can have her send you his number. His name is Maddox."

Yeah, I know his name, and my dad does not need to know why I already have Maddox's phone number saved in my phone. "Sure, Dad. I'm going to take the train that gets in at 11:05. Have Judy send me his phone number."

I'm going to hell for lying to my dad. I know most people passed this dubious landmark back in high school, if not sooner, but my dad and I were always close, even before my mom died. I don't remember ever lying to him. But on the scale of little-white-lie to giving-dad-a-heart-attack, I'm aiming squarely for a benign falsehood in this case.

"Sounds good, honey. I'll see you Thursday."

I end the call and move back to the stream of text messages that came in while I was out with Justin.

JJ

I'm home. I'll give you details when you get back.

I'm just at the bar. Be home in like 30.

JUDY

> Hi Judy, I'm going to take the train that gets in at 11:05. Thanks for offering to pick me up. If you send me Maddox's number, I'll coordinate so we get there at the same time.

I'm going to hell.

MADDOX

> The date was good.

> You home now?

> Yeah.

I've barely hit *Send* when there's an incoming call from Maddox.

"Tell me about the date," he starts, without even saying *hello.*

I lean back on my pillow with the phone pressed to my ear. "It was good." Maddox does not need to know that there wasn't a spark. I don't even need a spark.

That's made up, and the last time I fell for a spark, it wrecked me.

I just need a guy like Justin, who looks nice, is polite, and won't rip my heart out in front of my entire family.

"Oh?"

I snort. "Don't sound so surprised. I can be a good date."

Silence.

When he speaks, I swear his voice is lower. "You're an amazing date, Holly."

I push away the butterflies that swarm in my stomach when he drops his voice to that octave. "Anyway. My dad told me to ask your mother for your phone number so we can coordinate our arrival times on Thursday. So I, uh, texted her to ask for your number."

His chuckle vibrates through the phone. "I knew you'd want my number eventually. So you didn't tell them you already had it? And exactly why you had that number?"

"No! And before you ask, I already feel like shit for lying to my dad. And to your mom. But they don't need to know about anything that happened between us. It's in the past." I chew on my thumbnail.

"I won't spill, Holly. But between you and me?"

He pauses, and my stomach flips again when his deep voice comes through the speaker. "It's not in the past."

Heading to a bar on Thanksgiving eve might have been a mistake. No, it was definitely a mistake.

This place is crawling with college students home for the holiday. We can barely make it to the bar. I'm tempted to call it a night and head home, but Justin texted me earlier today.

JUSTIN

I had a great time last night. If it's still cool, I'd love to see you tonight.

I sent him the name of the bar again and the time we'll be there. So now we wait to see if he follows through, although it might not be fair to expect him to find me in this sea of people.

I look around for any spot to sit, or even lean against the bar. Most of the seating is taken, but then I see Justin. Amazingly enough, he's managed to snag a booth toward the back with enough empty seating for all three of us. He waves when I catch his eye.

I drag JJ over to the booth and we slide in, balling up our jackets in the one empty spot.

"Justin, this is my friend JJ." I motion to my best friend. She shakes his hand as she silently judges him.

Justin ignores her critical gaze and smiles. "Nice to meet you, JJ. And it's good to see you again, Holly. Can I grab you guys some drinks? Holly, do you want a vodka cranberry?"

Um, swoon. He remembers my drink order.

"That would be great, thank you." I smile in what I hope is a flirty way.

"Dirty martini, but I'll come with. That's a lot to carry," JJ says.

The two of them slide out of the booth, leaving me to guard our real estate. I hope they like each other, because I'm hoping this thing with Justin goes further. A, because he seems like a genuinely good catch, and B, I have fifty grand riding on this.

Over our second round of drinks, it's more and more obvious that Justin and JJ are getting along. He's laughing at her jokes, listening attentively to her stories.

I cross my fingers. I can't date someone that JJ doesn't approve of, so this night is key.

The vodka makes its way through me quickly. I excuse myself and slide over JJ to slip out of the booth. The restrooms are in a hallway toward the back of the bar, and I pick my way through the crowd. I need to make this speedy before JJ tells Justin any embarrassing stories.

The line for the bathroom isn't exactly short, but it takes only about ten minutes for me to do my business and check my makeup in the smudged mirror. In the dim light, my lipstick seems faded, so I add another coat of the deep berry color and check my reflection again. There. I look like a girl who wants to be kissed.

I slip the tube back into my purse and wash my hands again before I pull open the door with a paper towel and exit, tossing it in the trash before the door closes. There are a million germs on public bathroom door handles.

I bump into someone as I round the corner. "Sorry," I mutter, before I look up.

"Hi." Maddox looks down at me. Are his eyes darker than normal?

Butterflies flurry in my stomach, and I tamp them down. There will be no butterflies where Maddox is concerned. Plus, I'm here with another guy. *Pull it together, Holly.*

"Oh. Hi. I didn't expect you to be here tonight. JJ

and I are at a table over there." I gesture vaguely with my hand. Why am I so flustered? This doesn't bode well for having to spend the day with this man tomorrow.

"I see you brought your date. Or is he JJ's date?" Maddox's eyebrows lift.

Um, can you feel the awkwardness right now?

I make what I hope is a nonchalant gesture with my hand. "No, um, he's mine. My date, I mean. That's all. Do you, uh, want to meet him?"

Maddox shakes his head slowly, his gaze never leaving my face. He places a hand on my upper arm and pivots us, then takes a step toward me.

I take a step back, then another until my back is against the wall. Maddox is just a little too close, his gaze a little too hungry. My breath quickens.

"You shouldn't be with him," he says, before he dips his head and captures my lips.

His kiss is nothing like Justin's. It's not sweet or respectful.

It's harsh, dominant, like he's staking a claim. His lips press hard against mine, demanding entry. When I part my lips, he slips his tongue inside.

I moan into his mouth. His fingers grip my chin as he assaults my lips, and every other thought disappears except one.

I want him.

Then he steps back. "I'll see you tomorrow," he says, like he didn't just turn me to a pile of mush. He plants a kiss on my forehead, turns, and walks into the crowd.

I slump against the wall, my knees too weak to hold me upright. I stay like that for a minute, then go back to the bathroom to hide the lipstick evidence of our kiss that's smeared all over my face.

10

MADDOX

olly's kiss lingers on my lips with the sweet taste of her favorite cranberry drink. Maybe it wasn't fair of me to interrupt her date, but then again, it's not fair of her to be looking for her soulmate when I already know where he is.

I'm right here.

I waited for her text, her phone call, some communication to express her anger after I pushed her up against the wall in the back of the bar and kissed her. My phone's been silent all evening, though. I don't mind if she's confused about her emotions. In fact, I'd kind of like her to be. That's the perfect situation—we head to Thanksgiving dinner with her uncertain of her feelings for me versus her date. Because he won't be there, and I will, ready to be sweet and attentive and everything she deserves.

It's too late to text anyone now and expect a reply, but I type out a message to Cam, who's a night owl and probably still up.

CAM

You taking the train out to Ardmore with us tomorrow?

Three little dots appear right away, confirming my theory. Cam is nothing if not predictable.

Cam

Sure. What time?

We're taking the 10:45 from 30th street.

Ok, see you there.

I stare at my phone for a few more minutes before I accept that I'm not going to hear from Holly tonight. I plug it in and set it on the bedside table after setting an alarm for eight in the morning.

My eyes have barely been closed for a few seconds when I jolt awake at the sound of an alarm. Is there a fire? I look around, frantic, before I realize the shrill banshee-like noise is emanating from my phone.

It's my alarm. Like, to wake up.

My heart races in my chest. Jesus, do people do this every day? It almost gave me a heart attack. This can't be a healthy way to wake up.

I slide out of bed and run a hand over my face. I turn off the awful buzzing sound and check my text messages. Nothing from Holly about last night. Fuck. I'm going in blind today. I have no idea what's going through her head.

HOLLY

Good morning, beautiful. Do you want me to pick you up on the way to 30th street station or meet me there?

When I slip out of the shower ten minutes later, there's no response yet, but I know how to get one.

HOLLY

> I'll plan on picking you up unless you tell me otherwise, okay?

> I'll meet you there.

I grin. So she is pissed at me, although she hates being told what to do regardless of how she's feeling toward me. Good. Anger is a strong emotion. So is love. They're not that different from one another. And with any luck, she's not mad at me, but at herself, too. That we can work with. It's easier to go from anger to love than from indifference to love.

Now, don't think I'm a total dick trying to manipulate her emotions. I'm not. I'm stacking the deck in my favor, sure, but I'd never force anything she didn't want. My goal is just to make sure she has all the available information before she decides. Like I've said, I'm all in here. And you don't go all in unless you're fairly certain things are going to work out in your favor and are ready to do what whatever it takes to to make sure it does.

I wave across the terminal to Holly, who looks about as happy to see me as a bear emerging from hibernation. Maybe she got woken up by a banshee screech of an alarm, too.

"I got your ticket," I say when she gets close enough to hear me without my having to yell.

She snatches it out of my hand. "I can buy my own ticket, Maddox."

"I know. But I was here, and I bought it. I got one for Cam, too." As I say his name, I see him approaching and raise my hand in a wave.

Holly's arms cross over her chest, her gorgeous face twisted in a frown. She narrows her green eyes at me.

"Hey. If you're mad at me about last night, I'm sorry. Do you want to talk about it?" I'm not actually sorry, not one bit. It was an amazing kiss.

She blows out a breath. "I'm... it's not you. Not entirely, at least."

"Oh?" I tilt my head.

She shakes her head. "No. It's—" She breaks off as Cam approaches us.

"Hi, you must be Holly. I'm Cam, Maddox's best friend." Cam offers his hand.

Holly shakes it but doesn't offer any pleasantries.

I start us moving toward the train platform. "Do you want to talk about it on the train? I'll get rid of this wing nut." I motion to Cam, who groans good-naturedly.

She gives me a small nod, looking between Cam and me. "I mean, if he's okay with it."

Cam is already slowing down, putting some distance between us with an understanding smile. "I'll sit far away with headphones."

We settle into our seats for the thirty-minute ride out to the Main Line. That's what it's called, this section of the Philadelphia suburbs, because the main rail line goes through the towns. Never said we were a creative bunch. Cam, true to his promise, heads in a different train car after giving me a wink, and Holly and I manage to find a seat where we can sit next to one another.

"So?" I give her leg a nudge with my thigh as the train starts to move. "What's going on?"

She twists her hands in her lap. "I'm not sure. I'm all confused about Justin. He seemed so good on paper, and he was so sweet on our first date. He texted me after the date. He met up with me at the bar last night, but then something... changed."

I wait for her to keep going, but she doesn't. "What do you think changed?" I prompt.

She shrugs her shoulders.

"Did you eat the mayonnaise and hot sauce abomination in front of him?"

A smile finally plays at her lips. "No."

"Did you tell him about your theories about getting abducted and murdered?"

The smile gets bigger, then disappears. "I did, actually. And he was really cute at first. He likes SVU and shows like that, too. I thought it was something we had in common."

I wait.

"He was all sweet, but then later in the evening, he was kind of... distant, I guess. Like he was trying to be nice but not encourage another date or something." She lets out a sigh.

I study her expression. She looks frustrated, sure, but it's not the look I'd expect if she were really into someone and it didn't pan out.

That look I'm familiar with. I've been seeing it every day in the bathroom mirror.

"Holly... did you actually like this guy?" There

were two people doing the kissing last night. She didn't kiss me like a woman who was falling for someone else.

She chews on her lip and wrinkles her forehead. "He was a good prospect. I have to bring someone to the wedding who won't—"

She breaks off and looks away.

What's she so scared of? There's more here. This isn't just about Justin or even about me, is it?

Holly leans her head back on the headrest and closes her eyes. "Maybe I'm reading too much into it. Maybe he was just tired or something and I'm over-thinking it."

"You? Overthink something? Never," I deadpan.

She smiles, her eyes still closed, and I let it go for now.

My mother's car is waiting outside the Ardmore train station when we descend the stairs from the platform. But instead of my mother, a ball of energy jumps out of the driver's seat and hurls herself at us.

"Maddox! Holly! It's so good to see you!"

Holly's eyes go wide as Addie wraps her in a hug. "Um. Hi, Addison. Happy Thanksgiving."

Addie beams at her and turns to me, offering a

quick hug. She looks at Cam, who is hiding behind me and Holly.

"Hi, Addison," he says, making no move to hug her.

I may have once told him something like that if he touched my baby sister, I'd cut his dick off. Cam's a good guy, but Addie's my little sister. Plus, the first time they met, Addie was like thirteen or fourteen. She was way off limits back then, and even though she's twenty-seven now, I don't see any reason to encourage the two of them.

She ignores the slight and pulls Holly toward the car. Cam and I follow a few steps behind. The ten-minute drive from the station to my mom's house is filled with chatter, mostly from my sister. After a couple of minutes, Holly warms up a bit and is more like herself, or at least the version of herself I know.

It strikes me that I only know part of her. It makes me want to spend every minute with her, see all the different versions. We all have different selves for different situations—friends, family, work—and I want to love all of hers.

"So, did you two get to know each other a little on the ride over? It's nice that you were able to coordinate your trains," Addie says to Holly, who is sitting next to her in the front passenger seat.

"Uh... yeah, we got to talk a little," Holly manages.

I kick Cam before he can open his big mouth. He of course knows the whole story, right down to the bet I made Holly. He also knows better than to spill this, but he's got a long history of putting his foot in his mouth.

Addie has moved on to a long soliloquy about the types of food Mom made, and the desserts, and how Mom and Josie got in a big fight last night because Josie wanted to make the pies and Mom was offended because she thought Josie didn't like her pies, but Josie just wanted to help. I'm not sure Addie takes a breath through all of it.

By the time she pauses enough to let someone else speak, as well as presumably to take that breath so she doesn't pass out while driving, we're pulling into the driveway of my mom's house.

The white colonial is where I grew up, for as far back as I can remember anyway, and it's still exactly the way it was twenty-five years ago, right down to the tulips that line the front path during the spring and summer. Right now, there's just the remnants of the garden, the dirt buried solid under a dusting of snow.

Addie parks the car in the driveway, perilously close to Josie's Highlander. She squeezes out the driver's side door and waits. Holly steps gracefully out of the car, the bottle of wine she brought in her hand. Both of them watch as Cam and I spill out of the passenger side of the back row like two overgrown toddlers.

I knock on the door frame as I push open the front door. "Hello? Mom? Josie? We're here."

A chorus of voices comes from the direction of the kitchen. I pivot that way, motioning with my head for Holly to join me. She and Cam both follow me until Holly spies her dad sitting in the family room and hurries off to talk with him.

Mom and Josie are already squabbling in the kitchen over who should peel the potatoes. Every year this comes up, and every year I vow that I'm going to buy another peeler just to avoid this situation. I don't know why one of them doesn't just use a knife.

"Josefina Consuela Anderson!"

My mother's voice raises to her "I'm trying to yell" volume, which isn't much louder than most people speak in a crowded room, but it's always had the effect of grabbing our attention when we were young. She's normally so soft-spoken that it's a big departure from her usual tone and in turn gets results.

Unless the kid you're yelling at is thirty-six.

I step between the two of them. "Hey, Mom,

Josie." I give them each a hug. "No one brought another peeler this year?"

Josie rolls her eyes. "Not my fault. We flew down from Boston. You can't take a peeler on a plane."

Cam gives my mother a quick embrace. "Thanks for having me, Mrs. A."

"Oh, any time, dear," my mother says, hugging him back. "Happy you're here."

I steal a carrot from one of the cutting boards and pop it in my mouth. My mom smacks my hand as I go for another.

"Stop stealing food. You'll eat at four," she scolds.

I chew the carrot and swallow. I'll grab more when they're not looking. "How come you're not decorated for Christmas yet? You usually have the tree up by now."

It was the first thing I noticed when I walked in. My mom loves to decorate for Christmas, but I don't see a single mini tree or piece of tinsel anywhere.

My mom looks toward the hall to the family room, then focuses on the potatoes she's peeling. "It's... well, it's not really my stuff to tell. But Robert said that Christmas was always really special to Holly growing up, and her mom made it this big deal, all magical. And he said that since his wife passed, Holly hasn't wanted to celebrate. So I just figured I'd wait. I don't want to make her uncomfortable, and I don't want her to think I'm trying to replace her mom."

She shrugs and looks up just in time to catch me stealing another piece of carrot. She points the peeler at me like a weapon. "Get out of my kitchen. And buy your own damn tree this year like the adult you supposedly are."

"And *then* he knocked his front teeth out during a Little League game." My mom points to a picture of me in the album that's perched on Holly's lap. "He was playing with the bat, holding it in his mouth for some reason, and he knocked those teeth right out!"

Holly laughs as she looks at yet another embarrassing photo of me. This one features me in a baseball uniform, blood decorating the front of it. The teeth hadn't been quite ready to come out.

"Aw, Maddox, you look adorable." Holly smiles at me. "Did he cry, Judy?"

My mom snickers. I raise my eyes to the heavens. Jesus, don't they have pies to make or potatoes to mash? Why are we focused on old photo albums?

I reach for the album on her lap in an attempt to snatch it away. "Why don't you look at pictures of

Addie or Josie? I'm sure their childhood photos are a lot cuter than mine."

Holly smirks. "Oh, I'm sure we'll get to theirs soon." She turns the page.

My mom claps her hands. "Oh, I remember this! The fourth-grade spelling bee!"

Holly is trying and failing to hold in a laugh. "Maddox, you were a spelling bee champ? I mean, I believe it. You look... smart."

Yeah, I know that's a dig at the nerdy look I rocked back then. But in my defense, I... actually, I have no defense. I chose those glasses that gave me bug eyes and at the time, I thought the hairstyle I was going for was super cool. In hindsight, a bowl cut—that I slicked down with so much styling gel that there were blue flakes in my hair—might not have been the height of fashion, in the Nineties or any other era.

"You know, I can't wait until we go to Robert's house. I'm sure he has plenty of old photos of Holly for me to look at," I deflect with a pointed look at her.

Addie joins us, sliding onto the couch with the other two women. Holly is now sandwiched between Addison and my mom, the photo album still on her lap. It hits me how seamlessly Holly fits in with my family. Not like Ashley. My ex-wife was only ever after one thing, money, and my family saw right through it.

It took me longer to realize, but seeing Holly with Mom and Addie makes me see that Holly is nothing like Ashley.

The attention of all three is squarely focused on me and my shortcomings at age ten, which is not where I want it to be. It's sweet and cozy and all, but also completely embarrassing to look at these pictures.

I need to derail this train *stat*. Or get it back on the tracks, or whatever metaphor is appropriate here.

Unfortunately, the most apt metaphor is probably one about a train crash, where you can't look away. None of the three can tear their gaze away from the pages. They don't even look at me as I stand from the couch and walk out of the room in search of a beer.

11

HOLLY

Being squished between Addison and Judy is more comfortable than I would have imagined, both physically and emotionally.

Addie isn't much taller than me, and she's the kind of thin that's delicate rather than angular. Judy's body is soft and warm, and every time I brush against her it's like being wrapped in a hug. And the couch is worn and lived-in, the kind that sucks you in when you sit.

But it's their friendly demeanor that has really set me at ease. I don't let people in easily, but Addison and Judy are doing a solid job at breaking down my walls.

The holiday decorations might be missing, and I'm sure my dad had something to do with that, but the feeling here is one of warmth, love, and family. It's the feeling I remember from holidays with my mom.

It's almost enough to make me forget why I need an acceptable date for this wedding in the first place.

We've been thumbing through photo albums of Maddox for almost half an hour now. The man himself disappeared about five minutes ago, but seeing these photos of him as a young boy is making me see him in a whole new light.

It's strange to realize that people had an entirely different life before you met them. He wasn't always this confident, self-assured guy who wins poker games for a living. He had the same gawky phase I did, although God knows I never used as much hair gel as he did.

Addison is as much fun as Maddox told me. I'm still a little thrown off by the idea of having a sister, let alone two of them—three if you count a sister-in-law, Josie's wife—but the idea is growing on me.

The brother, not so much.

Judy looks at her watch. "Oh, goodness, the turkey!" She shoves the photo albums toward Addie and me and shoots up from her seat.

Addison giggles as her mother scurries out of the room. "Every year. She gets involved in things, forgets to baste the turkey, and apologizes up and down about how it's going to be dry and ruined. And every year it's the best thing you've ever tasted."

"Do you think she needs help in there?"

Addison waves her hand in dismissal. "She's got it handled. Josie likes to insert herself into the cooking process and Mom gets flustered, and they end up fighting, even though I have a suspicion that Josie is the one who bastes the turkey when Mom forgets. It's the same every year, Thanksgiving and Christmas. Honestly, Josie and Chris have been going to Chris's parents' place the last few Thanksgivings to keep the peace. I'm glad they decided to come here this year, bickering aside."

Maddox hadn't told me much about his sister Josie, so I've had to piece some things together. All I knew was that she lived in Boston, along with her wife, Chris.

Addison whispered to me that the two of them have been going through fertility treatments, trying to get Josie pregnant, and that's why—Addie's words, not mine—Josie is being bitchy. Addie and Josie seem like polar opposites to me. It's not just their looks, although that's part of it, with Addie's coppery red hair and pale skin a sharp contrast to Josie's tan skin and black hair. It's their entire personalities.

I mull over the information about Josie and her fertility treatments as I turn the page in the photo album, flipping to a picture of three kids and two adults in front of a Christmas tree.

I look closer and pick out the three Anderson children next to Judy and a man with a kind face that must have been their dad. There seem to be a bunch of photos from certain times, then it seems to jump to a year later, with nothing in between. That's three kids for you, I guess. You take pictures when you can remember.

As an only child, I had the nonstop attention of both my parents all the time. There are probably two million pictures of me buried in photo albums in the house.

Before I can ask, Addison takes the album from my lap. "I barely remember this. It was Christmas. I think I was maybe four. Maddox was probably ten or eleven, and Josie would have been about twelve. The two of them were always close because they were so close in age. I always looked up to them so much." She shrugs her shoulders, then looks up at me. "I think that's why I'm so excited for Mom to marry your dad. I've always wanted a sister my own age, and even though it's not like we're all moving in together as a stepfamily, it's kind of..."

She trails off, but I know what she means. I smile

gently. "I've always wanted siblings. It was kind of lonely with just me and my parents."

Addie reaches out and gives me a side hug as raised voices from the kitchen start to filter into the family room, along with the mouth-watering smell of turkey. "Let's go break up this fight, eh sis?"

I brought a bottle of wine to share, but by the time we start putting out appetizers, it's long gone, along with two bottles of chardonnay, which Judy claims were somehow involved in the cooking of the turkey and thus "don't count" toward the total wine consumption.

I'm just glad we took the train, because no one is going to be in a state to drive after this.

The dinner is just as delicious as Maddox promised. Whatever Judy did to the turkey with that wine had to be magical, because it's juicy and delicious.

"Butter," she whispers to me at one point. "That's the secret. Lots and lots of butter."

Or maybe it was the turkey basting fairy, also known as Josie.

I let my gaze travel around the table, taking everything in. Judy is at the head of the table to my left, confident in the position she's assumed as the matriarch of this group. My dad is sitting across from her, way down at the other end. On my side of the table, Maddox and Cam are helping themselves to more and more food, while the girls across from us are politely wiping their mouths.

Other than Addison, who is taking another piece of turkey. I think she might be my favorite Anderson, but it's stiff competition. Every so often, she looks up at Cam, who's directly across from her, and I can't quite read her expression. Is there history there?

Our Thanksgivings were never like this when I was growing up.

It was Christmas that was always the main event. Mom would make a small turkey, and the three of us would eat it without much fanfare. We haven't even done that since she died. Why would two people need a whole turkey?

Chris and Josie are gazing at one another in adoration. Dad is making eyes at Judy. Addie has her head thrown back in laughter at something Maddox said, and he's elbowing Cam.

As I take it all in, I think the secret isn't butter at all. I think it might be love.

I reach for the white china. "I can do that, Judy."

Addison was right; Judy doesn't like to accept help in the kitchen. It seems like she's slightly more willing to accept help with the cleanup than with the cooking, although that's not saying much. So far, she's let me carry in plates from the dining room and stack them on the counter and has let me put the silverware in the dishwasher.

She shakes her head. "Oh no, I have it, dear. Why don't you go see what everyone is up to? We have a bunch of board games that we like to pull out after Thanksgiving dinner."

This is enough to pique my interest. I do love board games.

"Are you sure I can't help?" I say slowly.

Judy smiles as she loads another delicate plate into the dishwasher, angling it in a particular way that I wouldn't have figured out. "I appreciate it, Holly. I'm just picky with how I load the dishes. You'll have more fun with the kids, anyway."

I ask one more time to make sure she doesn't want my help, then leave the kitchen when she shoos me away. I follow the voices to the family room. They've set up a card table in the center, and my dad, Maddox, and Josie are playing a card game.

"Holly! Good, we need another person. Are you

up for Code Names?" My dad puts his cards down on the table. He's the one who fostered my love of games from a young age—board games, card games, you name it—and he loves nothing more than trouncing me in whatever game we're playing. I think I get my competitive spirit from him.

A smile plays on my lips. "I don't want to interrupt. What are you playing?"

"War," Josie responds, holding up her stack. "I'm winning, but this game takes forever. Now that we have four players, I'm good with switching to Code Names if you are, Maddox." These are the first words she's really spoken to me, but at least she's okay with me joining the game. Maddox was right; she really is a tough nut to crack.

Maddox doesn't object, and ten minutes later we're set up with a fresh drink in front of each of us and the Code Names cards set out.

Josie taps a finger on her chin. "Let's see. I think we should split up Holly and her dad to be fair. Should we do boys against girls?"

I'm about to cast my vote in favor of that when Maddox opens his big mouth. "I want to be on Holly's team."

I whirl around to look at him, shooting bullets with my eyes.

Maddox shrugs. "What? You seem like you'd be good at this kind of game."

He's not wrong. I'm really good at Code Names, but you need a good partner for this.

Josie has already settled into her chair across from my father, solidifying herself as his partner, so it's too late. This still gives me a chance to beat my dad, though, so I'll take it.

The premise behind Code Names is that you're spies, and you have to get your partner to guess as many of your code words as possible by giving them a one-word clue. It works well if you know your partner, so they understand where your mind would go for a given word. I've always had better luck with another girl as my partner when I'm not paired with my dad, since girls think differently than boys.

I study the game cards that are laid out. I'm going to give the clues first, so Maddox will have to figure out what I'm thinking.

We're totally going to lose.

"Rain. Four." I hope Maddox gets my use of *rain* as a homophone, like *rain* and *reign,* because him getting all the words right hinges on it.

He strokes the hair on his chiseled jaw, his dark eyes taking in the cards laid out on the table. He leans back and takes a sip of his beer, then sets it on the table before pointing to cards one after the other. "Cloud. Weather. Umbrella." He pauses, and I worry he's going to end his turn.

We're on round five, with two wins each. This is crunch time. *Don't fuck this up, Maddox.*

He looks me right in the eye, winks, and says, "King." He points to the card.

I nod, smiling as I put the markers over the ones he got right. We're down to one card to guess, and Dad and Josie have three. I cross my fingers.

The entire group is now gathered in the living room, other than Cam, who left about an hour ago to head back to the city early. Judy and Addie are heavily engaged spectators, leaning over the board to whisper suggestions, while Chris, Josie's wife, is reading a book and paying no attention to the building rivalry.

Josie guesses the two clues that Dad gives her, and now we both have one card left. He has to get this one. Our clue is Venus, which should be simple, right? Just say *planet* and move on. But *mercury* is on there, too, and I don't want him to guess that.

I think. Venus razors? Would he have any clue? Or maybe Venus flytrap, but I don't know if *flytrap* is technically one word or two, and I don't want to lose on a technicality.

Did I mention I'm a little competitive?

Venus di Milo, but only an art history nerd like me would get that. Men are from Mars, Women are from Venus. I chew my lip as I try to figure out which one he'd guess.

Is Maddox most likely to know about women's hygiene products, self-help books, classic art, or botany?

These are not the choices I was hoping for.

He has two sisters, so hoping for the best, I say, "Razor."

Shit.

Now he's looking at me like I have two heads. I should have said *flytrap*. Or *milo*.

Maddox silently reaches out and taps *Venus*.

I let out an excited *whoop*. "Yes! That's it. We win! Best out of five!"

Maddox chuckles. "You didn't want to say flytrap?"

We clean up the game as we finish our drinks. Josie pulls Chris out of her chair and the two head silently upstairs to bed. Addison gives everyone a hug before she disappears up the stairs, too.

I stand up and stretch. "We should get going. Thank you so much for having us, Judy. This was so much fun."

"Of course, Holly. It was my pleasure. You're welcome here any time, you know." She looks down at her watch and frowns. "I think you two missed the last train, though."

I pull out my phone to check the time. There are a few texts from JJ and one from Justin, but my attention is focused on the time. 11:44. She's right. The last train left Ardmore at 11:13. Crap. Now what do we do? It's going to be expensive as fuck to get an Uber all the way back to the city.

I look at Maddox. He looks way too happy about this for some reason, which makes me suspicious.

"Darn. Do you mind if we stay here tonight?" Maddox asks cheerfully.

"Oh, of course. I think it's just your old room that's available, though. Josie and Chris took her old room, Addie's in her room, and Robert and I..." Her cheeks color slightly as she trails off, but they're in their sixties and both have been married before and have had kids.

No one is under the illusion that they're saving

themselves for marriage here. But also, no one wants to think of their parents... you know.

Hold on. Forget Dad and Judy sharing a bed.

Did she say there's only one bedroom?

Maddox nudges me. "You can take my room. I'll show you where it is."

12

MADDOX

The walls of the staircase are lined with pictures: posed graduation and holiday photos, candid shots of all of us growing up. I sweep my gaze over them as I walk up the carpeted stairs, gesturing for Holly to follow me.

"Come on. I'll get you a toothbrush."

"We can't share a bed!" she hisses from behind me.

I don't say anything. I had planned to take the couch, but I'm interested in hearing her logic.

"You know we can't!"

I peek back at her again and hold back a smirk. She has the most adorably flustered expression on her face. Why does she care so much about our family knowing there's something between us? "Don't worry. I'm sleeping on the couch. I'll just make sure you're settled first."

The bathroom is directly at the top of the stairs. My mother redecorated after we all left for college, and now it's got kind of an Under the Sea theme. Blue and beige wallpaper, and seashells everywhere. I pull two new toothbrushes out of the drawer. The pink one I set on the counter next to a soap dish. The dish is shaped like a starfish and holds three tiny seashell-shaped soaps which, knowing my mom, are for looks, not use, just like the little decorative towels. There's a container of liquid hand soap just behind it.

I pull the green toothbrush out of its packaging. Holly has been standing in the hallway, watching, and I wave her in. I hand her the pink toothbrush while she takes in the decor.

"Judy likes the beach, huh?"

I nod. "The toothpaste is right there," I mumble through a mouthful of minty foam.

Holly follows my pointed finger to the travel-sized tube and puts a stripe of toothpaste on her brush. She squeezes in the center of the tube—I cringe internally —and then puts it down without putting the cap back on. I watch as a tiny bit lands on the counter. I wipe the tube and put the cap on. She's not really watching, so I quickly squeeze the contents of the tube up from the bottom. Sue me. I like things neat.

We stand there together for a minute, brushing, and I take a moment to revel in how normal this all is. How easy things are with Holly. I just need her to realize how right we are, her terrible toothpaste squeezing technique aside.

My childhood bedroom is right next to the bathroom. I push the door open for her, but she waits in the hall-way, so I go first.

Holly follows me in, her gaze moving around the room, which has thankfully been updated since I was a teenager. It smells better now than it did back then, too.

The walls are painted a calming shade of grey with white accents and framed black and white landscape photos on the walls. The centerfolds and baseball posters that I hung up with thumbtacks directly into the drywall are gone, along with the holes in the wall from said thumbtacks. Mom made me help her cover them up before she had it painted. The room is neutral now, a place for guests.

There are still some old shirts of mine in the white

dresser that faces the foot of the bed. I dig out two of them, sniffing to make sure they smell either like laundry detergent or like I smell now, rather than teenage boy. I toss one to Holly.

"You can wear this to bed. It's clean."

She catches it and clutches it in front of her like a shield. Fuck, I don't want her to be uncomfortable. I didn't exactly correct her right away on the one bed thing, but I was joking there, at least mostly.

I step toward her and plant a chaste kiss on her forehead. "Goodnight, Holly." I leave her standing next to the bed while I return to the bathroom to change, leaving my jeans and sweater on the countertop for the morning.

When I emerge in my boxers and the t-shirt, ready to head back downstairs for a long night on the couch, her door is cracked open, the light off. I'm about to put a foot on the stairs when I hear her voice.

"Maddox?" It's soft, barely audible in the creaking old home.

I turn around, listening at the door, and she says it again. The door squeaks as I push it open enough to enter, and again as I close it behind me.

"What's up, Holly?" I ask, my eyes adjusting to the darkness of the room.

She's lying on one side of the bed, the covers pulled

to her waist. In the king-size bed, she looks so small, and her full breasts are outlined against the soft cotton of my old shirt.

"Today was really fun. I've never really had Thanksgiving with a big family," she whispers.

I grin, even though she likely can't see it, and sit on the edge of the bed. "This was small compared to some of our Thanksgivings."

"Judy seems like she really enjoys the holidays." I can hear the smile in her voice.

I lean back on the bed and position myself on my side on top of the covers, facing her. "She does. She goes all out for Christmas. Usually, the decorations come out the day after Halloween."

Oops. Wasn't supposed to share that part.

"That's what my mom always did, too." Her voice is soft. "Did Judy... did she hold off on decorating because of me?"

I scoot toward her enough to brush a piece of hair away from her face. "I don't think she meant for you to know, but yeah. She knows how much Christmas meant to you and your mom. She doesn't want to overstep or make you uncomfortable."

Her voice is soft. "She's an amazing lady. I really like her."

"She likes you, too, Holly. We all do." I touch her

shoulder. "I really like you, too." I rub her arm, feeling her muscles relax beneath my hand.

"I..." she starts, then seems to reconsider. "Thank you for listening, Maddox. I like talking to you."

I rest my hand on the curve of her hip. "That's what I'm here for, babe. I'm here for you."

She smiles. I move my thumb back and forth over the bony prominence of her hip.

"Now roll back the other way so I can go sleep on the couch. If you keep looking at me like that, I'm going to kiss you." I want to respect her wishes, but a man can only be pushed so far.

Holly's gaze meets mine in the shadows of the room. She doesn't roll away from me. She doesn't move at all except to dart her tongue out to run it over her lips, and all my blood rushes to my dick.

Fuck me.

I give her another second to move away, to keep us from doing something we might regret, and she doesn't. Her breathing gets heavier.

"Holly," I whisper, my voice strained.

I grip her chin between my thumb and forefinger and lean in for a kiss. Our lips meet, and it's like coming home. Comforting and familiar and exactly right. This time, she's controlling the kiss as much as I am. She sucks my lower lip into her mouth, nibbling lightly, and I swear to God I almost come right there.

I move my hand down to her side, slipping under the covers, and then slide it under the hem of the over-sized t-shirt. I trace the line of her hip up to its crest and dip down at her waist.

Our tongues tangle as I play with the elastic of her panties, pulling lightly before I move up her body. My fingers move along the underside of her breasts. I run my thumb over one nipple. She lets out a gasp, and I do it again.

"I—we can't," Holly says, breathless, but she moves closer and kicks the covers down, revealing long, bare legs.

I let out a groan. "Fuck, Holly." I roll us so she's on top. For once I need her to be the one in control here. She needs to want this.

My arms are loose around her as she lifts up her torso, keeping her pelvis firmly on mine, the pressure on my erect cock making it hard to hold back. Hell, it's making it hard not to come right now.

"We can't have sex," she whispers, her body still moving against mine, testing my control.

We're barely separated, just the fabric of my boxers and the thin cotton of her panties. It's taking every-thing I have in me not to push the barriers aside so I can sink deep inside her. The memory of our first night haunts me—her tight pussy clamping down on my length, the slick heat of her channel. *Fuck.*

"We don't have to have sex," I say, even though that's exactly what I want. I lift my hips, grinding against her. She lets out a soft moan that makes me even harder.

She pushes her groin against me again, and I need more. More pressure, more movement. More *Holly.* I grip her hips and move her against me.

My cock slides between her legs, the fabric between us providing friction and making all of this feel naughtier than it is. Or maybe this is exactly as naughty as it feels. It's the closest I've been to Holly since that first night, and that one time is what I've been fantasizing about since then. Even without penetration, I'm practically ready to come already just from being so close to her and hearing her soft cries.

Hell, who am I kidding? I'm ready to come any time Holly looks at me. I'm like a high schooler over here.

I keep moving her back and forth over my cock, angling my hips to press against her clit. She bites her lip and lets out a soft whimper as I push against the bundle of nerves.

"Oh god, Maddox," she whispers, and her words are my undoing.

I clench my jaw as I control her riding me, forcing myself to hold off until she comes, but I don't have to wait long.

Holly's head drops back and her eyes close as her body tightens. Her jaw clenches, holding in any sound until she lets out the tiniest noise as she rides me harder through her orgasm, and I come in my boxers like a goddamn teenager.

I wait until Holly's breathing evens out before I pull the covers up over her and pull a new pair of boxers from the dresser, thanking God that my mom never made me move all these spare clothes home. The door squeaks when I open it, and I pause, but she doesn't move. I tiptoe down the stairs, avoiding the spot that creaks, and settle myself on the couch with a throw pillow under my head and a knitted afghan over me.

The family room isn't exactly the place to spend the night if you want to sleep late, and I'm reminded of this when I crack my eye open to find Mom and Robert sitting in the armchairs across from me with coffee mugs in their hands.

"What time is it?" I groan, rubbing my eyes.

"Six thirty! The early bird gets the worm!" Mom chirps.

The early bird would get something thrown at it if I had a suitable projectile. I fold the afghan and place it over the back of the couch after I sit up.

"You sleep okay?" Robert asks over the rim of his coffee.

I *did*, until you two lovebirds woke me up. "Yeah, it was fine. Thanks for letting us crash here. I'll wait until Holly is up so someone can drive us both to the train station." I stand and stretch. "Is there more coffee?"

"Of course. Creamer is in the fridge." Mom waves her hand in that direction, like I don't know where the kitchen might be after living in this house for something like thirteen years. "But I asked Holly to come with me and the girls to do the last fitting for my wedding dress. Addie or I will drive her home after, so you don't have to wait around."

I was hoping for some more one-on-one time with Holly to see where she stands after last night, but it looks like that's not going to happen today, or at least not this morning.

The coffee maker is still half full when I enter the kitchen, and I fill a mug to the brim with morning sludge. No need for creamer to dilute the caffeine, which is what I need right now.

I lean against the kitchen island and take the first sip. Just the aroma wakes me up a little, and I'm almost functional when a pounding on the stairs cuts into my thoughts.

Addie shuffles into the kitchen in an oversized sweatshirt and pajama pants. Her red hair is up in a messy bun, although some of the strands have escaped and are framing her face. She's only a morning person when she wants to be, and apparently today isn't one of those days.

She doesn't acknowledge my presence while she grabs a mug from the cupboard and fills it with coffee, then adds a liberal splash of creamer.

She drops into a kitchen chair and takes a few gulps before she finally looks at me.

"Are those your boxers in the bathroom trash can?"

13

HOLLY

I stare at my reflection in the mirror, trying to make sense of everything.

I kissed Maddox last night. I fucking dry humped him.

I'm not sure what it says about me that I came harder from over-the-clothes action with Maddox than I did from sex with old boyfriends.

I shake my head. This is Maddox. My friend. My *future step-brother*. I can't think of him like that. His mother invited me to go help her with her wedding dress fitting today, for God's sake. I have no business getting horny over her son.

What would my family think?

I haven't seen most of my extended family since *The Incident*, as JJ has taken to calling it. I'm not sure that label really covers the abject humiliation and devastation of that day, and I'm not doing anything to put myself in a position like that ever again.

I can only imagine if I showed up to the wedding in a relationship with Maddox. The judging looks. The conversations in the ladies room: *She's such a nice girl. Poor thing. It's a shame she has such bad taste in men.*

My clothes are still folded in a pile on the counter where I left them last night, next to Maddox's. I pull them on and leave Maddox's t-shirt in their place next to his pants and sweater, which are folded so nearly they look like they belong on a display in a retail store.

The pink toothbrush is sitting in a cup next to the seashell-themed sink. I brush for more than the recommended two minutes, ruminating on everything that happened last night before I spit and rinse my mouth out.

It appears that I'm the last one to wake up and make my way downstairs, although I'm one of the only ones who put on actual clothes. Judy and Dad are dressed normally, but Maddox, Addie, Josie, and Chris are still in pajamas, with everyone lounging on furniture in the family room, all comfortable with one another.

If only my extended family were like that. Heat

rises in my cheeks as I see Maddox's boxers, definitely different ones than he wore last night.

I saw the other pair in the bathroom trash this morning. God, I hope no one puts that together.

"Coffee is in the kitchen, dear," Judy calls from her spot in an armchair in the family room.

I just offer a nod, unprepared to deal with humans before caffeine. Especially humans who may or may not have found Maddox's boxers in the bathroom trash can. How does one even explain that?

I open cabinets until I find the mugs, piled high in mismatched stacks. The first one I can reach says *#1 Mom*. It's chipped and obviously well loved. I mix coffee and creamer together and carry it into the family room just in time to see Addie launch a pillow at Josie, bringing an amused smile to my lips.

Judy twirls in front of the mirror with the grace and giddiness of a twenty-something girl. "What do you think?"

"Perfect!" Addison claps her hands.

She does look perfect. The dress is white of course, but knee-length. It's modest with a high boat neck and elbow-length sleeves. It's not a traditional wedding dress other than the color, but as Judy and my dad keep reminding me, this is the furthest thing from a traditional wedding.

"It's gorgeous, Judy. Dad's going to love it," I say.

Josie is refilling her champagne glass with sparkling water across the room but gives us a thumbs up.

"How about a veil?" The salesperson circles around Judy. "It would pull the whole look together."

"Oh, I don't know." Judy looks at Addie and me. "This isn't a first marriage, obviously. I don't want to be too flashy."

"Why don't you try it on?" I suggest. "You don't know until you try. And the only thing that matters is that you and Dad are happy. It can be as flashy or un-flashy as you want."

She beams at me and ducks her head so the salesperson can put on the veil. When she stands up straight and looks at us, the effect is stunning.

"Oh, Mom," Addison gushes at the same time that I say, "Oh, Judy," both of us in the same breathy tone of voice.

We look at one another and dissolve into giggles. So, this is what having a sister is like.

Josie plops back on the sofa next to Addie. "I think it's better without the veil."

Addison elbows her. "It looks good. And it only matters what Mom wants."

And I suppose this is the other side of having siblings.

The two start to bicker while I pretend to be extremely interested in something on my phone.

"Girls, stop it. I'm going to get the veil. Thank you for your opinions," Judy says firmly, stopping their squabble as she steps down from the dais and pulls the veil off. She hands it to the salesperson before walking back toward the couch where the three of us are sitting. "Addie and Josie, go get more drinks for all of us. They need to do the final alterations before I take this off."

Josie holds up her half-full glass, but Judy waves her off to refill. As the two girls walk across the room away from us, Judy settles herself next to me. "Now, Holly. Tell me. How are things in your life?"

I was not anticipating a heart-to-heart. I'm not really prepared for one right now. I go for the work angle. "Things are good. I'm happy with my job. My roommate and I have been best friends for years, so it's good to still live with her."

She nods. "How about your love life?"

Damn, Judy. Cut right to the chase, why don't you?

I shrug. On the one hand, bonding. On the other, she probably doesn't want to hear about the dirty things Maddox and I have been doing.

"It's... okay. I'm working on finding a date for the wedding." An appropriate date. A date who's not my future stepbrother.

I don't think Judy would care, honestly. She doesn't seem like the type to judge. And maybe after this whole wedding thing, I can work my shit out and be okay dating Maddox. Maybe.

She nods sagely, like she knows more than she's saying. "Well, that's nice. Anyone in particular you're interested in?"

I shrug again. She's going to think there's something wrong with my shoulders. "Sort of, but it's... complicated. He's not someone I should be dating, so..." I trail off, spreading my hands wide.

Judy tilts her head. "You know, I met your father almost two years ago."

This is news to me.

Addison and Josie return, each carrying two glasses: champagne for Addie and me, sparkling water for Josie and Judy. Addison hands a glass to her mother, and Josie hands one to me. I take a sip, enjoying the feel of the bubbles in my mouth.

Judy sips at her glass, then sets it on the low table

in front of us. "Robert and I only started actually dating about eight months ago, though. Even though we were attracted to one another when we first met, I felt like it was wrong initially. We were both fairly recently widowed. It seemed like I was cheating on my husband. It felt like people were judging me for moving in on someone who'd lost his wife so recently." Judy pauses to take a sip of her sparkling water. "The point is, Holly, that sometimes things are right even when they might seem wrong from the outside. Society tells us one thing. But we have to follow our hearts."

She stands up and moves back to her position on the dais, glass still in hand.

Addison and Josie slide back into their spots on the couch.

"What was that about?" Addie asks.

I shake my head. "I don't know." This is one hundred percent a lie. I know exactly what it's about.

I'm just not sure I'm ready to hear it.

JJ is engrossed in some game on her phone when I burst through the door of our apartment. She looks up briefly, something on her face unreadable. It almost looks guilty, but I don't have time to dissect that right now.

She gives me a wave. "How was Thanksgiving?"

"Interesting. Infuriating. Confusing." I plop onto the sofa across from her.

She taps something on the phone, then places it on the coffee table. "Do tell. I thought you were going to be back last night, by the way."

I blow out my breath. "Yeah, so did I."

And then I tell JJ the whole story. How we missed the last train of the evening. How I slept in Maddox's old bedroom, how we laid there and talked until I fell asleep. I rolled over at some point during the night and realized he wasn't there, but he'd pulled the covers up over me.

I leave out how we dry humped one another to completion.

JJ's eyebrows rise higher with each successive detail. When I finally take a breath, she stands up and walks toward the kitchen.

"JJ?" I call.

"We need chocolate for this." She returns a few minutes later with one of the Hershey's bars we stock-pile in the freezer.

I unwrap it and crack off a piece of frozen choco-late. "So? What do you think?"

"I..." JJ looks almost nervous, which is not an expression I'm familiar with when it comes to her. She's basically cultivated her personality around being assertive and straightforward.

"JJ?" I ask, confused.

She swallows the piece of chocolate she's chewing and washes it down with a sip from her ever-present water bottle. "Okay. You know I love you, right?"

I nod. "Right back at you."

"And I want what's best for you."

This sounds like she's about to break up with me or fire me or something. What the hell is going on?

"What is it that you really want, Holly? The incident aside. The family drama and all that shit aside. What do you want? Or who?" Her gaze is so intense that I almost have to look away.

When she puts it that way, it's actually not a hard question. "Maddox," I say softly. "But I can't—"

She shakes her head. "We're not talking about everyone else right now. I know you have stuff in your past. We all do. God knows I'm as fucked up as anyone else. But I can excuse some of your stupid behaviors because I understand where you're coming from. Maddox doesn't. I think you owe it to him to tell him."

I can't, though. Even thinking about the incident

makes my cheeks flame and my stomach curl into a ball. What would Maddox think of me if he knew?

"I know," I admit. "And I know he's a good listener. It's just still so humiliating."

She puts a sympathetic arm around me, and I lean into her shoulder. "You can do this. And Holly?"

I sit back up and look at her. The expression she had before is back. Nerves or anxiety or something decidedly un-JJ-like.

"Please talk to Justin. I got to know him a little the other night." Her gaze darts away, then comes back to me. "He's a good guy. If Maddox is who you really want, let him know. Don't string him along."

She's right. I sigh. "He sent me a text yesterday. He wants to meet to talk."

JJ puts more chocolate in her mouth and chews it slowly. "I think that's a good idea."

I dig through my purse to find my phone and send Justin a text, hoping I don't regret this. He was the closest to an acceptable prospect for a wedding date.

At this point, the bet is weighing on my mind, but it's not the reason I need a date. I'm willing to forgo the money if I have to. I just need to save face in front of my family.

JUSTIN

Hey, I hope you had a good Thanksgiving. Did you still want to meet to talk? I'm free later today or tomorrow.

His reply comes back a few minutes later.

Hey. Yeah, let's meet this afternoon. How about the coffee shop on Twelfth and Market? Right by Reading Terminal?

Sure, that works. See you then.

The Cheshire Cat is a popular hangout, with squishy couches and funky decorations. It's nearly empty today, and I'm confused until I remember that colleges are on break right now.

I spot Justin at a table by a window. He waves to me, standing up as I walk over.

You can do this, Holly. Just tell him you have feelings for someone else. He's a nice guy. It'll be okay. You're doing the right thing.

"Hi, Justin," I say.

He opens his arms, gathering me in a hug. "Hi, Holly. Good to see you." He releases me. "Do you want a drink? It's on me."

He's such a gentleman. It makes me feel worse for what I'm about to do.

"Sure. I'll take a hot chocolate, please. Thanks." I slide into the empty seat while Justin heads to the counter to place my order.

Once he settles back across from me, both of us with steaming mugs in front of us, he looks at me with a serious expression. "So, um, it's been really fun getting to know you. And I want to be upfront with you."

Huh. This is not going the way I imagined.

Justin keeps going, his face earnest, "I met someone recently, and I'm interested in pursuing a relationship with her. I like you a lot, but I see a future with her. I don't want to be a dick, and I'm so sorry. I don't date multiple people at the same time, though, and I just don't want to lead you on."

I guess I'm supposed to feel disappointed, or rejected, or something, but I came here to tell him the same thing. "I appreciate your honesty, Justin. Thank you."

"Well, maybe don't thank me just yet." He winces slightly. "It's your roommate."

Well, then. I consider this for a minute. They actually seem like a great match, now that I think about it, much more than Justin and me. We have a lot in common, but JJ and Justin seem to share this need for upfront, honest communication and this same strong moral code.

And maybe there's a spark between them, the one that was missing between Justin and me.

I smile at him. "I'm not mad. I actually think you two make a cute couple. I think you and I are really similar, so it makes sense that my best friend likes you and me both. And to be upfront with you, I have feelings for someone, too."

Justin smiles. "Friends?" He reaches his hand across the table. "And I promise you, nothing has happened between me and JJ. Neither of us would do something like that to you."

I know JJ wouldn't go behind my back like that, but I appreciate his reassurance anyway.

I take his hand and shake it. "Friends."

14

MADDOX

There's something I'm not seeing. I pace back and forth. If I keep this up much longer, Cam will have a hole in his living room carpet.

"Dude. Talk to her." Cam started ignoring me after about half an hour of pacing and complaining. He's got the TV on now and is flipping through streaming options.

"I have, man. If there's one thing I do well, it's talk. Put that undergrad psychology degree to work and all that. But there's something she hasn't told me. I don't know what it is, but whatever her hang-up or past is, it's keeping us apart."

It's been over twenty-four hours since I took the

train back to Philly from my mom's house. Holly stayed behind to do something with wedding dresses with my mom and sisters. I can only imagine the conversations they had in my absence.

"She seemed into you all day on Thanksgiving," Cam points out.

I shrug, dropping onto the couch next to him. "She was, or at least it seemed like it. We actually talked after everyone went to bed." I don't need to tell him everything. "She almost said something on the train, too. About bringing someone to the wedding who won't do something. But then she clammed up, wouldn't tell me what she was talking about."

Cam scratches his chin. "She has a roommate, right? Are they close?"

"Inseparable, from what Holly's told me." I haven't spent much time with JJ, but I feel like I almost know her from all the stories Holly tells.

"Think she'd tell you?"

I let out a sigh and reach for the bowl of pretzels on the coffee table. "Maybe. I don't want to go behind Holly's back. But I get this sense that she's hurting somehow. I just want to fix it."

I shuffle the cards, folding them into a bridge that snaps them together with an oddly pleasing noise. I then cut the deck and deal out two cards to each of us.

Blake picks up his cards, studying them. "How was everyone's Thanksgiving?"

This is his favorite tactic. Get people talking about something other than the game. It distracts them, and he can usually read the inflection in their voices to get a sense of how strong their hand is.

I shrug as I look at my hand. "It was fine." My jaw tightens a bit. I've gotten good at knowing exactly what I'm showing on my face, and this time I'll let it slide. Because I'm looking at a great set of cards—king and ace, both spades—but my mind is on Holly.

Miller tosses chips into the center. "I had Chinese food."

"You should have come out to the Main Line with us. We had Maddox's mom's turkey. It was fucking amazing." Cam folds, placing his cards face-down on the table.

"Yeah? How's your sister?" Blake asks. He adds his chips to the pile.

I try to kick him under the table, but he's too far away. "Off limits, asshole. To all of you." Addie was eleven when I left for college. In my mind, she's still eleven, or close to it. It's a tough mindset to change.

We keep playing, dealing out cards and studying the hands. My head isn't in the game, and it's killing me to lose to these guys. This is the one place I can separate everything else from what's going on in front of me. If I play like this, I may as well drop out of the Vegas tournament I have coming up soon.

A buzzing from my pocket distracts me even further, and when I pull it out and see a text from Holly, any illusion that I was paying attention to the game vanishes.

I fold, placing my cards on the table, and stand. "I have to take this."

Cam raises his eyebrows in interest, but he doesn't say anything.

HOLLY

Can we talk?

I call her, and she answers on the third ring. I know she was holding her phone, so it makes me wonder why she wasn't ready to answer as soon as I called.

"Hi, Maddox," she says, a slight waver to her voice. "Am I interrupting something?"

She could interrupt every poker game I play for all I care if she needs something. "Not at all. Just playing poker with the guys. How was the dress fitting with my mom?"

Her voice relaxes as she starts to fill me in about the dress and the veil my mom chose. There's genuine happiness there.

She fits in so well with my family.

"So I, um, talked to Justin. The guy I went out with the other day." The nerves are back, and now I'm nervous.

Please don't pull back again.

"I..." She trails off, and I wait.

There's a moment of silence.

"Holly? You okay?"

"Um. Yes. Actually, can we talk in person? Maybe dinner?"

I silently fist pump. *Finally.* A dinner that I didn't have to beg her for or coerce her into. Maybe we're making progress. If she'll let me in, help me understand what's going on with this last wall between us, maybe there's a chance.

My phone rings just as I step out of the shower. I check the caller ID and swipe to answer.

"Hi, Mom. What's up?"

"Hi, honey. How are you?" Mom starts off with her usual pleasantries.

"Good, just getting ready to go out." I'm hoping she'll take the hint and make this quick, but this is my mom we're talking about. Brevity is not one of her many virtues.

"Oh, good. Well, I won't keep you. I wanted to touch base about the wedding."

She will one hundred percent keep me on the phone, but I play her game for a bit. "Yeah?"

The wedding is still three weeks away. I know for a fact that she did the dress fitting. She told me about how they're doing cupcakes, not cake, and that those are ordered. The catering is all set up.

What's left to talk about?

"You know it's going to be a simple ceremony, and we're not doing bridesmaids and so forth."

"Right," I say, trying to follow. Can I trim my beard without her realizing I'm multitasking? I could focus, but I'm sure she'd hear the buzzing of the electric razor. Mom picks up on everything. I walk into the closet with my phone still pressed to my ear.

"But I was wondering, would you walk me down the aisle and give me away?" She sounds so hopeful.

I stop looking through my shirts and pay attention. "Of course I will, Mom. I'd be happy to."

"Thank you, honey. That means so much to me." She sniffles a little. Probably tearing up, if I know her. "Also, speaking of the wedding..."

What now?

"Do you have a date?"

Ah. Now we've moved on to the interrogation.

"No, I don't have a date yet, Mom. I'm working on it." I pull a shirt off its hanger and slip my arms into it, then start to button.

"Okay. Well, just be patient. Sometimes great things take a little time." With that, she disconnects the call, leaving me staring at the phone in my hand.

I pull up in front of Holly's building just before six. I'm expecting to have to go fetch Holly from her apartment or wait for her to come down, but she's waiting in the lobby and stands when she sees my car.

She slides into the passenger side and buckles her seatbelt. "Thank you for picking me up."

Her gaze is on her lap. I rest my hand gently over hers that's resting on her thigh and give it a squeeze, then bring it back to the gear shift to pull away from the curb.

The ride to Mama Maria's, a pizzeria about halfway between our two apartment buildings, is short, and we're lucky enough to find on-street parking close by. Once we're out of the car, she lets out a heavy sigh, breath fogging in front of her in the chilly air.

"I'm sorry. I'm just in kind of a weird mood." She shrugs her shoulders.

I offer her my hand. "It's okay. Let's go in where it's warm and you can tell me what's up. I'm a good listener, remember?"

That elicits a small smile from her.

We're seated in a cozy booth toward the back, with a view of the brick ovens they use to cook the pizzas. The open flame makes it feel warm and inviting.

I wait until we've gotten our drinks and placed our order for a pizza to split. Once the waitress moves away from our table, I tilt my wineglass toward Holly. "Okay. Spill. What's going on that you didn't want to tell me over the phone?"

She chews on her lower lip. I'm learning that it's one of her tells; she does it when she's nervous or unsure of how to say something. "You know how I went out with Justin?"

Yeah, I remember. I wanted to punch his lights out. "Sure. Why?"

"Well, I talked to JJ after I came back from the dress fitting with Judy. Your mom is amazing, by the way. I love her."

I let her stall to put her at ease. There's no rush. "Everyone loves my mom. She likes you, too."

Holly nods slowly, her fingers tracing the rim of her wineglass. "So... JJ asked me who it is I really like. If I actually like Justin."

My heart thuds in my chest. *Please say it's me.*

She takes a sip of her wine. "And I realized... I don't. He's a lot like me. Too alike, probably. I met up with him, and it turns out there's someone he wants to pursue as well."

I pick up my napkin and put it on my lap to give my hands something to do. "I guess that makes it easier to make your decision then too, right?"

"Kind of. But the person he wants to pursue is JJ."

"Your roommate?"

She nods.

"Did something happen that night you were all at the bar?"

"No. He's actually a gentleman, it turns out. He just got to know her. He asked for my blessing to date her." She shrugs and takes a sip of her wine as the waitress drops off our order of mozzarella sticks. "Maybe he's one of the last real good guys, you know?"

I dip a mozzarella stick in marinara—close enough to ketchup to be a solid dipping sauce—and point the fried cheese at her. "He's not the last good guy, Holly. There are more out there. I promise." I bite off the half that's covered in tomato sauce, then double dip.

Holly smiles, her first genuine smile of the night. "You looked just like JJ when you did that. She points her food at me when she's making a point that she's really serious about." She looks thoughtful. "Maybe she and Justin really are a good match, you know?"

"Well, if so, I'm happy for them."

Holly chews on a mozzarella stick. Without dipping it in the marinara, I would like to point out. We all have our shortcomings. "I still need a date for the wedding, though. Someone who's not... you know." She nods her head, like she's trying to convince herself.

Maybe a public restaurant isn't the time to go digging into someone's deep dark secrets, but then again, there's no time like the present.

I wipe my hands on the napkin in my lap. "Holly,

what's the real story here? I know we made the bet and all, and it was a shock to find out our parents were together. I get it. But seriously. There's another reason you don't think we can be together. What's the real thing keeping us apart right now?"

15

HOLLY

A lump rises in my throat, keeping words from coming out. I take a sip of water, trying to gather my courage, but it goes down the wrong way and I end up coughing for several moments.

When I can breathe again, I'm not any more ready to talk about it. JJ is right, though. I owe him this.

"So, three years ago..." I start.

Maddox nods encouragingly. "That's when your mom died, right?"

"Yeah. Right around the holidays. I told you that part, I think. But before the accident, I was dating someone. And..." The feelings start to rush back. My stomach twists, unwilling to share all the embarrassing details. "Anyway, he was a jerk, and he came to Mom's funeral, and I was humiliated in front of my family. I heard my aunts talking about me in the bathroom. And I haven't seen most of my extended family since then, but I can't bring a date to the wedding that they're going to judge. I can't go through that again."

Maddox's brow creases. "You think they'd judge you if you went with me as your date?"

"I just... yes. And I know it doesn't make sense, and I don't want to go into more detail right now. I just felt like I owed you some explanation for why we can't date."

Maddox wipes his hand on a napkin and reaches out to hold my hand across the table. "Thank you for telling me."

How does he always know the right thing to say?

"Maddox, I—"

The waitress chooses that moment to bring our pizza, interrupting me, but I'm not even sure what I was going to say. I pull my hand away from Maddox's electric touch under the guise of giving her a place to put the pizza that looks way too big for two people.

I thank her, ostensibly for the food, but what I really want to thank her for is for saving me from saying something I can't take back.

❄

I didn't see JJ before I went to bed last night, but this morning she wasn't home when I left for work, either. It's not uncommon for her to stay out all night or to go home with a guy, but I have a hunch that she's with Justin. He swore up and down that nothing happened before we talked, and I believe him. JJ would never do something like that to me. But I'm pretty sure they're full steam ahead now.

Justin actually called me yesterday, wondering where she was, so there's already some drama there. All good JJ stories have drama, and I can't wait to hear about this.

And since we share an office as well as an apartment, I'm going to hear about it sooner or later.

I balance the two cups of coffee, one in each hand as I walk down the hallway. At our office door, I stack one on top of the other and pray to the coffee gods that I don't drop them when I turn the knob.

She's not at her desk, but I place one of the to-go cups at her spot. I settle into my desk. It's eight a.m. That's a reasonable time to call people at home, right?

I flip open the folder of potential foster families and run my finger down the list. I have less than four weeks to find Julio a new home, or else he goes to a group home.

I call five different numbers before I finish my

coffee. None of them are available for a new placement.

My gaze wanders over to the coffee on JJ's desk. She's still not here. We wouldn't want it to go to waste, would we? It's not a latte, but it's caffeinated, so if she's not going to drink it, I'll gladly fall on that grenade. I shoot her a text while I work up the energy to keep calling families.

JJ

> You coming in today? I got you a coffee, but if you're out of the office today, I'll drink it and get you one tomorrow.

> I'm out doing home visits all day.
> It's all yours.

Awesome, thanks! Dinner tonight?

> *thumbs up emoji*

I snag the coffee from her desk. It's cooled off a bit since I brought it in, and it wasn't exactly piping hot after walking the two blocks from the coffee shop to the office in the freezing cold.

The staff kitchen holds a microwave and a fridge

filled with leftovers of questionable vintage. No one is in here this early in the morning, so it's also pretty quiet. I pour JJ's Americano into one of the mugs I keep here and pop it in the microwave, leaning against the counter while it counts down.

Four weeks to find Julio a home, so three weeks until the wedding. I know I made that bet with Maddox, and I want to win just because I'm competitive. But the idea of actually *dating* another guy is losing its appeal.

But there *is* fifty grand on the line. Fifty grand would be life-changing. I could put a down payment on a house. I could set something up for the foster kids I take care of. Maybe just for Julio.

If I had my own place, maybe I could take him in.

The microwave lets out a proud beep, and I take the steaming coffee back to my office, rationalizing this idea and bargaining with myself. I'll call the rest of the families on my list and do my best to find a place for Julio. If I can't find someone, I'll have JJ set up another date.

Shady? Maybe. I'll come clean with Maddox in the end. I will.

I just want to help Julio.

Forty families. I called forty families and not one of them has availability to take on another foster kid right now.

I get that it's the holidays, things are tight, and that he's an older kid who's going to be tough to place, regardless. But thinking of Julio in a group home for Christmas just tears at my heart. If there weren't a ton of red tape in the way, I'd offer to take him home with me right now.

Plus, I currently live in a two-bedroom apartment with a roommate who likes to bring home her fuck buddies. I'm not sure it's quite the nurturing environment that an eight-year-old needs.

I flip the folder closed, downtrodden. I feel like I've failed him.

This is a slippery slope and a dangerous pathway to go down. If I take things like this personally, I'll never last in this job.

This is what I do, not who I am.

I repeat the mantra four times to help it sink in.

Because if being a caseworker—being Julio's caseworker—is who I am, then every kid I fail to place, every child that ends up in a worse situation than the one we removed them from, is a personal failure, a judgment on me and who I am. And as my mentor told me when I started, that's the quickest way to burn out.

I lean back in my chair and close my eyes. Maybe one of the other caseworkers has a lead on a new family that's going to be available. I'll use my network, find something for him. I grab a purple sticky note off the closest pad and jot a note to myself to look into that. I stick it to my computer screen, next to two other notes to myself.

And since I didn't find a home for Julio today, I shoot a text to JJ, asking her to set up another date for this weekend.

JJ looks troubled from the minute I catch sight of her across the restaurant. Is something already wrong with her and Justin? She texted me half an hour ago and said she'd meet me at the trendy bistro, since we were both coming from work. Me from the office, and her from wherever she's spent her day with home visits.

I slide into the booth across from her as I pull off my mittens. She's ordered us both vodka cranberries, and I take a grateful sip, savoring the tart drink.

"I feel like I haven't seen you in days! What's new?" I sip my cocktail between sentences.

JJ looks to her left. I've never known her to avoid confrontation, so this is all new to me.

The restaurant is about two-thirds full, which isn't bad for a Monday night. The hum of conversations around us is a perfect, soothing background to our heart-to-heart.

"Well, um..." She can't meet my eyes.

Okay, we're going to nip this in the bud. I've never seen JJ so nervous, and she has absolutely zero reason to be stressed right now.

"Did Justin ask you out?" I look straight at her.

JJ finally meets my gaze, her eyes wide. "How did you..."

I give a sharp nod. "He asked me for my blessing. He's into you. He's a really good guy, with morals that rival yours. I support it, JJ."

She must have been holding her breath, because she lets one out and slumps slightly in her seat. "I was trying to figure out how to tell you. I never try to go for guys you like or that you've dated, but there's something about him." Her gaze snaps up to mine. "I didn't go behind your back, I promise. Nothing happened until after you talked to Justin, and he told me you were okay with it. But I still feel shady as fuck not talking directly to you about it. I promise Justin wasn't scamming on you that night at the bar. We just had a really good conversation when we went to get drinks and then again when you went to the bathroom. I swear, you're number one in my life. Guys come and go, but we'll have each other forever, right?"

I laugh as she finally takes a breath. "Of course, babe. You're my ride or die, plus my source for clothes that are way cooler than my own. I one hundred percent support you dating him, and I told him the same thing."

JJ picks up her glass and holds it up. "Thank you so much, girl. You're my person, forever. I appreciate this more than you know. And... I like him. I really do."

I snort. "Of course you do. He's basically me with a dick."

We clink glasses and dissolve into giggles before we can take a sip.

"But," I say, pointing to her when we've reined in our laughter, "I need you to set me up on a date for Friday or Saturday. Or any day. I have three weeks to find a date for the wedding. Tick, tock."

JJ laughs again as she pulls her phone out, looking much lighter than she did when I walked into the restaurant. "If you're still insisting on dating someone other than Maddox, I've got you. There are three guys that have been messaging you, wanting to get dinner.

Look at them and let me know if you have a preference."

She passes her phone to me, the three profiles lined up on the screen. I click on the first one.

Peter, age twenty-eight. Software engineer. Loves cats.

I exit out. Nope. Cats are a red flag for me. There's no way I'd be able to pretend to be into him, even for a day.

I click on the next one.

Kyle, twenty-three.

I look at JJ. "Really? Twenty-three?" Like that's going to play well in front of my family.

She shrugs.

I delete him as an option. I'm sure he's a very nice person, just like Mr. Cat Lover. But we're on a mission here.

Option three looks cute in his picture thumbnail. I click on it to zoom in. Zachary, age thirty. Perfect. I read through his profile. There's a photo of him with a dog. *Ding.* A photo of him out in nature, hiking. *Ding.* A list of things he loves—among them, true crime podcasts and crime TV shows.

Ding, ding, ding. We have a winner, folks. Great on paper and might just be willing to help me out.

I look at JJ. "Set it up."

16

MADDOX

The best and worst part of road tripping to Atlantic City for a poker tournament with your friends is, in fact, your friends. At least if they're like my crew.

The tournament starts Wednesday. Because of the mid-week start, we're not expecting a big turnout, and we're all hoping that will work out in our favor. Cam is driving his Subaru, and I'm praying to any god that will listen that the commercials are true.

The snow is falling in flurries, but Cam is driving as though it's a summer day in Miami. No regard for the icy roads or for the fact that everyone else on the road has slowed down considerably. He's pushing the speed limit and passing cars that dare to slow him down.

The commercials swear that this car is both good in snow and solid in a collision. I'm praying for the first and hoping we don't have to test out the second.

Next time, I'm driving.

"How are things with your chick?" Cam asks as he cuts off a Jeep.

"Jesus! You're going to give me a heart attack. Things are fine, same as they've been. Slow the fuck down." I cling to the little handle above the window.

I'm pretty sure the factories install them for this exact scenario, or for parents teaching their kids to drive. I remember my dad holding onto it when he was teaching me to drive around cones in the high school parking lot.

Cam laughs, moving into the left lane to pass a semi-truck. "So, you're not getting laid."

Blake and Miller chuckle from the backseat. I send them withering glares, and their laughter fades. "Not that it's any of your business, but I'm taking it slow with Holly. I'm respecting her boundaries. Good things take time."

Miller snorts behind me. I reach back to smack him but catch Blake's side instead.

"Ow! That wasn't even me, asshole," he protests.

"Pass it on. Anyway, the point is, we're fine. Things

are fine. Holly and I are fine." I realize too late that I said *fine* one too many times.

"So, it's fine?" Cam slams on the brakes as the car in front of us slows. Thank god for anti-lock brakes and snow tires. "I wasn't sure from your description."

My dad always trained me to never hit the driver, because you didn't want to distract them. I think he told me it was illegal, like turning on the dome light when someone is driving at night. I curl my hands into fists. Thirty more miles to Atlantic City, then this joker is getting a black eye.

Blake, ever the peacemaker, cuts in. "So. Cam. How are things with Ellie?"

"We broke up," he grunts.

At least the question shuts him up for now. I hadn't heard about this latest breakup, but it's one in a long series for the two of them. We're all waiting for him to cut his losses and leave her for good.

They break up and get back together at least once a month, if not more frequently. I have no idea what keeps him going back to her, and he won't tell me.

"So, we can set you up with someone?" Blake presses.

Cam frowns as he passes another sedan. "Fuck no."

I roll my eyes, but I'm just glad the focus has

shifted away from me. Miller and Blake move on to talking about the hotel rooms in Atlantic City, and I tune out a bit. It's always the same, after all. We book two adjoining rooms, two beds each. We fight over who sleeps where. Cam and I end up sharing one room, and Miller and Blake end up sharing the other.

Every. Single. Time.

I'm not even sure why we bring it up anymore.

"So, in other news," Cam says, putting his turn signal on, "I found a sweet gig for me and one of you."

This is news to me.

"Yeah?" I look over at him, but he's focused on the road for once.

"Yeah. They have this thing where they hire pros to teach people to play poker in exchange for a deal on the vacation package."

"And where is this gig, exactly?" I'm always up for something new, and it does sound like a good deal, at least on the surface.

"Cruise ship." Cam merges into the left lane again while I hold on for dear life.

I've never been on a cruise, but from the nausea that's rising in my stomach from the way Cam is driving, I can imagine I'd be the kind of person who gets seasick. "Maybe. When?"

"They run the cruises all the time, but there's a

bunch over spring breaks and such. I just signed up to be notified for openings. They usually want at least one pro and a dealer, so it's perfect for two of us."

HOLLY

What are you up to?

In AC for another poker tournament this weekend.

Oh. When will you be back?

Tomorrow, probably by like 6pm. Everything okay?

Yeah, everything's fine. Just wanted to see what your thoughts were on wedding presents.

...Shit.

You forgot, didn't you?

Yeah. But in my defense, I technically haven't been invited.

They're not doing invites. It's family only.

Okay, okay, I'll figure something out.

It's like two weeks away.

I bet Josie got something. I'll text
her and see if she'll make it be from
all of us. That's what she does
every Christmas for Mom's gift
when we forget.

The tournament is a bust for me. Blake picks up a nice win, and Cam ends up making some money on blackjack, some of which is going to go towards the speeding ticket he picked up on the way back to town.

Serves him right. I *did* tell him to slow down.

Cam drops me off in front of my building. I check my emails while the elevator climbs to my floor, deleting spam message after spam message.

This is how they get you. You get on a mailing list, and then it's just easier to delete the messages than to actually unsubscribe. So they keep coming, and you keep deleting, and then eventually you give up and make a new email address. I'm almost at that point.

The elevator doors slide open. As I'm unlocking my door, Hilda steps out of her apartment.

Hilda Johansson has lived in this building for something like twenty years. I'm sure there was a time when she let people live their lives without meddling. Probably. That time is long gone, though.

She lives for gossiping and involving herself in

other tenants' lives, and once you engage with her, she's like one of those insects that burrows under your skin and stays there like an irritating little parasite, something I wish someone had told me about five years ago, before I made the mistake of getting into a conversation with her once. Now she doesn't leave me alone.

"Hello, there. Back from a romantic getaway?" Her beady eyes scan me for anything she can use to gossip.

"No, Mrs. Johansson. Just a trip for work."

"Hmph." Her lips turn down. "I know a number of nice young girls. I could set you up with one of them."

Of course she could. She's been offering since I moved in here five years ago. I'd bet anything these girls she speaks of aren't interested in being set up, either.

"No thank you, Mrs. Johansson. I'm perfectly happy with my life as it is." I push the key into the lock, hoping she'll take the hint.

She never does, though, and this time is no exception. "A man needs a woman around the house. Who does your cooking and cleaning?"

Dear Lord in heaven, I just want a beer right now. I don't want to discuss my cleaning routine, my relationship status, or really anything else.

I force a polite smile. "I know how to clean, but

thank you. If things change, I'll be sure to ask you for recommendations for a nice girl to take out, okay?" I turn the key and push my door open, stepping inside and starting to close the door to indicate the end of the conversation. "It was nice talking with you."

She mutters something I don't quite catch as the door swings shut. I lean my back up against it. It's been an exhausting few days. The poker tournaments can take a long time, but when you're winning, it's invigorating.

On a losing streak, it's just draining.

I wasn't kidding when I told my neighbor I was perfectly capable of cooking and cleaning. The cooking I'm just adequate at, not having absorbed my mother's cooking skills the way Josie did. But I excel at cleaning. It's soothing, in a way. Meditative.

I'm feeling more calm now that I've scoured the kitchen counters and cleaned the sink. Everything smells like lemons and tidiness.

I remove a load of laundry from the dryer and settle on the couch with it. Then I pull a shirt off the top of the pile and fold it methodically while I watch the news, more for background noise than anything else. Even my jeans have a specific way that I like to fold them.

What can I say? I like control, and I like things to look nice in the drawers. Plenty of people do. There's a reason Marie Kondo is so popular.

I fold together a pair of socks and set them next to the growing pile of t-shirts folded into perfect rectangles, splitting my focus between the laundry and a documentary about pandas. Those big oafs are fucking adorable.

I pull another t-shirt from the laundry basket and shake out any wrinkles. I'm laying it on the table in front of me to fold it when there's a knock at the door.

This better be good to pull me away from the pandas. I hit pause and tiptoe to the door.

I peer through the peephole to find Holly standing there, her eyes red even in this limited view. Is she crying?

I pull the door open. She *is* crying, her eyes red-rimmed and her cheeks stained with tears, and the sight hits me like a gut punch. I want to kiss all her tears away and make everything better.

"Maddox?" she sniffles before I have a chance to speak. "Can I come in?"

"Of course, babe. What's wrong?" I hold my arms open, and she falls into them.

Her body shakes with sobs. I embrace her while we stand in the entryway, brushing her forehead with my lips. My heart hurts for whatever happened to her, but I don't miss the fact that I'm the one she came to. I'm the one she sought out for comfort.

"It's okay, Holly. I've got you," I murmur. I don't actually know that it's okay, but I'll make it my mission to fix it, whatever it is. I have no idea what got her to this point.

I *do* know that when I find out who's responsible for making her cry like this, I'm going to have a few choice things to say to them.

Finally, her sobs abate, but she keeps clinging to me like a lifeline as she sniffles against my shirt.

"Holly?"

She sniffles in response.

"Are you ready to talk about it?"

She pulls back and looks up at me, swiping at her wet cheeks with the back of her hand. I brush her hair back from her face, cupping her cheeks with my hands.

"It's—it was Jared," she says, and a new wave of tears starts coursing down her face.

17

HOLLY

It's been a shitty day. I'm no closer to finding a home for Julio, and the clock is ticking. To make matters worse, I had a court hearing today for a pair of siblings who were hoping to be reunited with their mother. She didn't show, and the judge had no choice but to permanently remove the kids from her custody.

The sheer, unfiltered grief on their faces still haunts me as I pour myself a glass of pinot grigio, trying my best to block out the day's events. I did my best, and it wasn't enough today.

I wonder if JJ's day has gone any better than mine. It's after 6 p.m. and she's not home, so she's either having a shitty day at work too or she's already at the bar. Or maybe she's out with Justin, enjoying life. If that's the case, I don't want to be the one to put a damper on her fun.

I carry my overly full wine glass to the couch. I can stream a few episodes of CSI and then go to bed early. Yep, that sounds like a fabulous Friday night.

I lift the remote and turn the TV on. I'm about to hit play when a knock sounds at my door.

I pause. I'm not expecting anyone.

There it is again, firm and insistent.

Maybe JJ forgot her key? I'm pretty sure she'd text me, though. I get up and make my way to the door—quietly, in case it's a serial killer—and look through the peephole.

Fuck. It's Jared. That's worse than a serial killer. I don't have the strength for this right now.

"Holly? I can hear you there. Open the door. I need to talk to you." His wheedling voice comes through the door, and I take an involuntary step back.

Double fuck.

I undo the chain and open the door a few inches. "What do you want, Jared?" I'm not scared of him. He's never hurt me physically. Honestly, if I could swing it, I'd love to see him out in public. Somewhere I can emotionally destroy him the way he destroyed me.

He flashes me that smile, the one that gets him out

of every possible consequence in life. "I'm back in town, babe. I missed you."

No. Fuck no. "Jared, I'm not interested. Go away."

He leans against the doorframe, looking way too sexy, but I'm not going to fall for it. Not this time. "Aren't you going to invite me in?"

What? "No fucking way Jared. You broke my goddamn heart. You humiliated me in front of the people I love the most. There's no way to make that right."

He doesn't look the least bit remorseful as he says, "Sorry, babe. I was messed up back then. I didn't have my priorities straight. I miss you. I want to give it another go."

I grip the door so hard my knuckles turn white. "You had your chance. You ripped my heart out during the worst time in my life. You don't get another go at it." Tears prick my vision. I grit my teeth. I will not cry in front of Jared.

I thought I loved him, once. We met during grad school, when I was working on my master's in social work and he was a PhD student in the biochem department. We were hot and heavy for two years, even talked about getting married. Then my mom died in the car accident, and my world stopped. He held me, talked to me like he cared enough to help me through it.

And then at the funeral, I caught him fucking my cousin.

Correction. My aunt caught them, and instead of stopping them, she came and got me so I could see what was going on. And then she told everyone else. My entire extended family was there when he defended himself, telling me it was because I was too rigid, that I was bad in bed. That he couldn't help himself, that it was my fault.

The last straw was when I heard my aunts talking about it in the ladies' room, when they thought I couldn't hear. About how there must be a hint of truth to what he was saying. How it must be at least a little my fault.

"I know I fucked up. I'm sorry. I wasn't the man you deserved," he says, but there's no truth there. He's not sorry. He just wants what he wants, regardless of who he hurts to get it. I didn't see his selfishness back then, but it's clear as fucking day now.

And that he wasn't the man I deserved just might be the first truthful thing he's said to me.

"And I know I don't deserve forgiveness. But I'm just asking for a chance to make it up to you." His eyes fix on mine, beseeching. "Please, Holly. I still love you. Don't give up on us."

I'm momentarily speechless. Don't *give up on us*?

Three years after he ruined me, he has the gall to say *I'm* giving up on *him*?

"Fuck you, Jared." I slam the door before he can make a move to keep it open. I want to sink to the ground with my back to the door, all dramatic like they do in movies, but there's a good half inch of space between the bottom of the door and the fake hardwood flooring, and Jared would see me.

So instead, I latch the chain and turn the deadbolt before I retreat to my bedroom, where I do a beautiful impression of a Disney princess by flopping dramatically on my bed and starting to sob.

For someone who didn't want to give up on us, Jared seemed to give up pretty easily. He knocked for a few more minutes after I slammed the door, then nothing. I gave it thirty minutes before I checked, and he was gone.

I should be relieved that he left. I'm not interested in talking to Jared, let alone rekindling anything. But now the emotions of that day—*The Incident*—are piling up and ready to come pouring out of me. I need to talk to someone, share some of these overwhelming feelings that are now spilling out of my eyeballs and, to some extent, my nose.

A text to JJ goes unread for almost fifteen minutes. I don't want to interrupt her if she's with Justin, anyway. Most of my other good friends have moved out of the city. They're good for a phone call, but I need someone here. Honestly, I need a hug. I just need to be held tight, wrapped in the safety of someone's embrace to shield me from everything that's weighing on me right now.

Addison is an option, but I don't know her very well yet. Definitely not well enough to show up on her doorstep. I don't want to bother my dad with this.

Before I've really thought it through, I've taken a cab the twelve blocks to Maddox's apartment and am knocking on the door.

I've held in the sobs until now, but when I hear his footsteps coming to the door, the dam breaks. When he pulls the door open, the tears are streaming down my face in fat droplets.

"Maddox?" I manage. "Can I come in?"

He pulls the door open wider, letting me inside, and I fall into his outstretched arms. His chest is strong and sturdy while I cry into it. He just holds me, kissing my forehead and murmuring reassuring words that I barely register.

It feels like forever before I finally pull it together and start to explain my meltdown.

Maddox's brows furrow. "Who's Jared?"

Right, I haven't told him about the guy who screwed me up for life.

"He's my-my ex. We were together for two years, back when I was in grad school. He—" The words stick in my throat.

Maddox waits patiently for me to pull it together. He doesn't jump in, and right now, I love him for that.

I pull in a deep breath. "He-he cheated on me. At my mom's funeral. It's why—" A tear runs down my cheek as the shame surrounds me.

Maddox's arms circle me again, and I lean against him for support, needing some of his strength right now.

"I'm sorry, babe," he says. "I apologize on behalf of men everywhere. We're idiots, as a general rule. But it sounds like this Jared isn't just an idiot. It sounds like he's a douche-nozzle of the highest degree."

I laugh through my tears. "You don't even know him."

"Don't have to. The very fact that he could look at

another woman when he had you tells me he has the brains of a squid. And the fact that he made you cry means he's an ass clown."

The giggling has surpassed the crying, and now I can't stop. "Brains of a squid?"

He shrugs. "Pretty sure squids are dumb. Or another stupid animal. Maybe a salamander. Or a koala."

I laugh so hard I snort, which makes me laugh even harder. My cheeks are hurting by the time I finally get a hold of myself.

I look up at Maddox as the giggles fade to a smile.

His lips are turned up slightly, but he doesn't look amused. He looks serious, but also caring. Sweet. The intensity of his gaze is intoxicating, and I can't look away. My mouth falls open slightly as he leans in. His tongue darts out and runs over his lower lip.

I'm not letting Jared win this time.

He may have been the catalyst that made me so sure I needed my family's approval, that made me care what people thought to the point where I'd try to walk away from someone as wonderful as Maddox. But I'm not letting Jared get in the way this time.

I reach up and hook my hand behind Maddox's neck, pulling him toward me and meeting his lips in a fiery kiss.

He lets me take the lead. When I press my lips firmly against his, he presses back even harder. When I open my mouth to deepen the kiss, he does the same. When my tongue explores his mouth, he sucks on it gently.

In this moment, it's exactly what I need. Reality comes back into focus as I regain some control over myself and my situation.

I pull back and look him right in the eye, holding his gaze as I rise from the couch. I tug on his hand. He stands and follows me as I lead the way to the bedroom.

The first time we were here, he was the one entirely in control. This time, it's me.

I pause once we're standing by his bed. I lift my shirt up and over my head, letting the soft cotton fall from my fingers to the floor. My fingers find the button at the front of my jeans, unbutton it, and slide the zipper down before shimmying them to my ankles. I slip my shoes off with the jeans and kick them to the side.

My breath hitches as I look up at Maddox. He's watching me with dark, half-lidded eyes. I reach behind me to undo my bra clasp, my gaze on him.

"Are you sure, Holly?" Maddox asks softly.

I nod as the bra falls to the floor. "I'm sure."

He draws in a sharp breath. His gaze runs down my body, his expression almost reverent. Being naked in front of boyfriends has always been uncomfortable for me. It's not that I have a problem with my body, not really. But I'm acutely aware that while my boobs are big, so is the pudge of my tummy and the roundness of my ass. I just prefer to get naked under the safety of covers.

With Maddox, though, I don't feel uncomfortable. I feel beautiful as he studies me.

I hook my fingers in the elastic of my underwear and start to pull them down an inch at a time. They may be just pink cotton bikini briefs, but his gaze makes me feel like I'm peeling off something sexy and lacy, something you'd find at La Perla instead of at a local discount store.

Maddox watches intently while the panties slide to the ground.

He waits until I step out of them and toe them toward the pile of clothing before his fingers grip the hem of his t-shirt and pull it up over his head. He shoves his pants to the floor and steps toward me in just his boxers.

My mouth goes dry. I've seen his body more than once, and every time it has this effect on me. The sculpted pecs and abs covered by a sprinkle of dark hair that coalesces into a line that disappears down into his boxers. His strong arms, his toned thighs. The large bulge between his legs.

His Adam's apple bobs as he swallows.

"Get on the bed," he says. His voice is dark, commanding, and I surrender my control to him.

I try my best to look graceful as I climb onto the mattress. I look over my shoulder at him. Does he want me on my back?

"Head on the pillows. On your back. Legs spread."

I do as I'm told. Maddox joins me on the bed, kneeling between my spread legs. He puts his hands on my thighs, just above my knees on either side, and pushes them even wider, his eyes fixed on my core. "Fuck, baby. You're gorgeous."

Oh my God.

My eyes roll back as he uses his fingers to part me, exposing me completely. He slides one long finger inside me.

"You're so wet, baby. I almost forgot how tight you are." He moves in and out while stars dance in my vision.

"Maddox. Oh god." I'm panting as I get closer to an orgasm, the sensations swirling together, making me dizzy.

He pulls his finger out and replaces it with two,

curling them up to press against the front wall of my channel, which sends an entirely new sensation shooting through me. Is this what people mean when they say the g-spot?

It must be, because I'm riding his hand like I'll never get enough as he murmurs dirty things in my ear. I'm so fucking close to a climax.

Every thought of Jared has evaporated. Every thought of everyone who's come before Maddox is gone. I've never experienced anything like this, the way he plays my body like an instrument, like he knows it better than I do.

"That's right, baby." He slips his fingers almost all the way out, pressing the heel of his hand on my clit. "Come for me, Holly. Right now."

He pushes his fingers back inside me and curls them against that spot again, and I'm done. My body spasms, all of my muscles tightening at once. I thrust my hips up, fucking myself on his fingers while the waves roll through me, one after the next.

When the orgasm finally recedes, I'm limp on the bed, my thoughts scattered. I'm barely aware of Maddox moving as he reaches over and plucks something from the bedside table, but I watch as he rips the foil packet open and rolls the condom down his hard length, and I need more. I need him.

He notches his cock at my entrance, his gaze locked on mine.

Then he dips his head, capturing my lips in a passionate, claiming kiss and driving himself deep inside me in one smooth move.

18

MADDOX

Holly's warmth surrounds me, gripping me tightly. I've never been this lost in a woman before. I drive forward into her as she gasps and her pussy clamps down on me like a vise.

"Fuck, Holly," I growl, thrusting into her harder. "So good. So *fucking* good, baby." Was it this good the first time we were together? This feels like coming fucking home.

"Oh God. Maddox." Holly's head tilts back. I kiss the spot on her collarbone where her neck meets her shoulder, nipping just a little at the delicate skin.

I pump into her with purpose, my hips slamming into her pelvis. I can tell she's almost there, and so am I, but I want this to last. I pull out of her completely.

Holly lets out a whine. I slide off the end of the bed and pull her toward me by her ankles, twisting her over to lie on her front as I tug her toward me until only her torso lies on the bed. Her legs are just long enough that she can reach the floor by standing on her tiptoes.

"Maddox. Please," she whines again.

I slap her ass, a pink handprint blooming on her creamy white skin, and slide into her. This angle lets me go deeper, hit her g-spot. She lets out a groan.

"Oh, fuck. Maddox, I'm going to come."

I pull out and slap her ass again. "You'll come when I tell you to."

"Oh God," she groans again, louder.

I notch myself at her entrance again and grip her hips with both hands. "You need more, baby?"

"Yes. Oh God, yes, please, Maddox." She moves her hips, trying to take me deeper.

I pull her back onto me, giving her what she needs, and she lets out a throaty moan. I piston my hips, driving into her over and over, and I can feel her start to tighten around me. I'm right there with her.

I reach one hand around and press on her clit as I thrust into her. "Come for me, baby."

I feel her pulsing around me when the orgasm

takes over. Her entire body tightens in a spasm as I drive deep inside her and come right along with her.

I half expect her to be gone when I wake up. Actually, who am I kidding? The odds are more like ninety percent the way things have gone between Holly and me so far. Two steps forward, one step back. But all that matters is that we're moving forward together, no matter how slow we go.

And when I reach out, her warm body is still next to mine.

She gives a little sigh when I slide my body next to hers. I wrap an arm around her and pull her close, her back to my front. She wiggles her ass against my groin, and like magic, I'm hard again.

I cup her cheek as she stands by the door. "I'll call you, okay? Don't overthink this."

Holly blushes as she tilts her head to lean into my hand. "Okay."

I don't believe her even a little bit. She's going to

go home and think of all the reasons she can to regret what we did.

"Seriously. You start to overthink this, or regret anything, you call me. We'll talk it through. Don't spiral."

She nods.

I pull her in for a kiss, finishing by brushing my lips across her forehead. "Text me when you get home."

I watch her as she walks down the hallway, waits for the elevator, and steps inside. I wave as the doors close, even though I'm not sure if she can see me. Once she's gone, I shut my apartment door and lean up against it.

We're there. I think we're there.

She came to me this time. She wanted it, the same way she did the first time we met. And it was better than that first time, at least for me. The connection was deeper. Even this morning, when things might have been warped by the harsh morning light, we were still on the same page, or at least it seemed that way.

Is this real? If she's willing to give this a shot, it seems almost too good to be true.

There's a poker tournament coming up, a big one, in Vegas. The guys and I are planning to go. This one has the potential to be a big payday, especially with the chance of picking up some more sponsors if I do well.

But now I'm rethinking everything. Maybe I shouldn't leave town right now. Maybe I should stay here, spend more time with Holly. Poker will always be there. If I mess things up with Holly, I'll regret it forever. I send a text message to the group to get a feel for what they all think.

CARD SHARKS

> Considering pulling out of the Vegas tournament next week.

The replies fly back almost instantly, fast and furious.

> Miller: WTF? Why???

> Cam: Bad idea, man. How come you're considering?

Blake: This is a big one, Mad. You're going to be shooting yourself in the foot if you pull out.

Cam: Is this about the girl?

Blake: What girl? The one you've been moping around about?

Miller: If you mess up your career because of a girl, you're going to regret it.

Cam: …unless it's THE girl.

Blake: Seriously, details, man.

Miller: I need more details too. Cards and drinks tonight?

Cam: Sure. We can meet at my place.

Fine.

Blake: I'm in.

Cam: Maddox, bring Doritos.

I toss the phone on the bathroom counter and turn on the shower. I should go to this tournament. They're right. It *is* a big deal, and potentially a huge payday, but only if I can keep my mind focused. My game has been off lately, so this could also turn into a huge disaster.

I feel like I've finally gotten to a place with Holly where we have a real shot, where she's given up on the bullshit idea of finding someone who will love her more than I will.

I step into the shower once the steam starts to billow out and dunk my head under the scalding spray. If Holly asked me, I could promise her that no matter how long or hard she looks, she won't find someone who will love her more than I will. Not because I don't think she can find someone who will love her. I absolutely think she will, and the idea terrifies me. I even think she could love them back.

But none of them will love her as much as I do. Like I said, I'm all in.

I spend the afternoon mulling over the events of the last twenty-four hours, taking a break only to go for a run and visit the store to pick up a bag of chips for tonight. I sent Holly one text—just one, I held back— and she hasn't responded yet.

I need advice. Most people probably have a trusted

source they turn to when they need advice or when they need to talk. I don't, though, not really.

My mom is a solid source of advice, but I don't want to entangle her in this whole thing. Plus, she's planning a wedding. She has enough stress, even though she keeps insisting that this is a small ceremony. Addie and Josie are also off the table. They're too close to things.

And who wants to talk to their sister about sex?

My sisters don't need to know about sex. They're pure angels as far as I'm concerned.

I need an impartial judge, and those are tough to come by.

I scroll through the contacts on my phone, hoping for inspiration. Not Cam or any of the poker guys. Not my college roommate. Not whoever Andrea is. I honestly can't remember.

Maybe a one-night stand? Probably, but I used to be the kind of guy who had one-night stands and then forgot all about the girl in question. I never called them again. Until Holly, that is. Thinking of her makes me even more certain that I don't need Andrea's number, whoever she is. I delete the contact, then keep scrolling.

There's one name toward the end that might be an option. I'm sure he'd give good advice, even if he's biased. Or he might murder me, but that's a chance I'm willing to take.

I hit *Send* and press the phone to my ear.

"Hello?" he answers on the second ring.

"Robert, hi. It's, uh, Maddox. Judy's son." I don't know why I'm so nervous. Actually, scratch that. I know exactly why I'm nervous. I'm on the phone with the father of the woman I'm falling for.

He chuckles. "Hi, Maddox. I know who you are. What can I do for you?"

"I have a question for you. Uh, more than just a question, actually. I need advice." I pace around my bedroom, needing something to do.

"I've got plenty of that, son. You get old, you start to want to share your wisdom with the world."

I squeeze my hand into a fist, then release. "It's about Holly." *Please don't murder me. It would ruin the wedding, and then my mother would murder me again.*

"Mmm?"

Oh, hell. No sense beating around the bush now. "I like your daughter, sir. We actually met before we knew you and my mother were engaged. I'd like to take things further, but there's something holding her back. Maybe something with her ex, but she won't tell me enough to let me help her. There's some reason she thinks we can't possibly be seen dating at your wedding."

Robert is silent for several moments. I hold my breath, hoping he's not checking his shotgun or something.

Finally, he clears his throat. "Maddox, I think you're a good man. I haven't known you long, but from what I've seen and what your mother has told me, I'd be thrilled for you to be dating Holly. And you're right, there are some things in her past you're going to have to work through."

He takes a breath, weighing his words carefully.

"At Marcy's funeral—my late wife—there was an incident with her ex. She doesn't know that I know the whole story, and it's her story to tell, but suffice it to say that my extended family is particularly gossipy and judgmental. I think Holly was at an extremely vulnerable place at that time, and she's conflated some of the grief and devastation she felt that day with how our family reacted to the events of the day.

"Now, I don't give a rat's ass about you being her stepbrother, as long as you treat my little girl right, and I think you will. And as critical as my family is, they mostly mean well, and we don't see them often enough to really care what most of them think. This wedding will be the first time most of them are in the same place since Marcy's funeral, and Holly probably won't see them again until her own wedding, if she even chooses to invite them."

As he speaks, the picture becomes clearer. The focus on the date for the wedding, one that looks good on paper. The horror at dating her stepbrother, at what people would think. And the absolute meltdown when Jared came to see her. He's the one who did this to her.

I want to make him pay for what he did to her that day. For the way he's made her question herself.

Now that I know, I don't care about her pulling back from me these last weeks, because I understand. It was never about me, and this is something we can get past. I don't take care if it takes weeks, months, even years.

19

HOLLY

JJ pounces on me as soon as I open the apartment door. "What did *you* do last night?"

I'm not in the mood for an inquisition, but there's no escaping JJ when she's on a mission.

"I... I went to Maddox's place." I try to walk past her, needing to brush my teeth and shower. It may be the weekend, but I still want to feel like myself rather than some washed-up, emotionally hungover version of me.

"And?" JJ presses.

I bite my lip. "And I stayed there. I'm back now." I want to talk about Maddox and my night with him, but I know I'll have to tell her the part about Jared showing up, and that part still hurts.

She slides her arm into the O I've created with my hand on my hip and steers me toward the couch. "Oh, my little horny BFF. Details, girl."

She drags me across the room, and her excitement is infectious, but I know it's going to come to a screeching halt when I tell her about Jared. I have to.

"Jared came over here."

JJ stops a short two feet from the couch. "That little fucking weasel?"

"Yeah, that one. I kicked him out, but just seeing him..." I swallow, take a deep breath. "Anyway, it fucked with my head. I needed to vent, and Maddox..." I hold my hands out, palms up.

Her eyes narrow. "Oh, that little fucker. Jared, not Maddox," JJ clarifies.

"Yeah. Fucking Jared." I sink down onto the couch. Wait a minute. "Did you talk to Justin? Or go out with him?"

JJ's cheeks turn red. I've never seen her blush in the four years I've known her, so that's saying something.

I let out a squeal. "Ooh! You went out with him! And?"

JJ's gaze slides toward her bedroom door before she pulls it back to focus on me, but I don't miss it. Looks like I'm not the only one who got lucky last night.

"Well, we umm..." JJ flounders. It's the first time I've seen her tongue-tied over a guy.

"He's still in your bedroom, isn't he?" I waggle my eyebrows.

JJ shrugs, but a little smirk spreads over her lips. "Technically, he came over this morning, not last night. But maybe we should do the polite thing and wait until he leaves before we talk about him."

I snicker. She has a point. Let the man do the walk of shame instead of hearing gossip.

"Let's talk about you instead. So, are you and Maddox a thing now? Are you finally giving in to what everyone else can see?" She raises a knowing brow.

I think I am. I'm still not over everything with *The Incident*, and I'm not sure I'm going to be able to openly take him as my date to the wedding. Plus, the whole bet thing. I like him. I really do.

So much so that I want to toss the bet out the window, if the fifty grand were just for me. But I've been thinking more about everything with Julio, and now I'm conflicted. I've loved Julio for longer than I've known Maddox. The kid needs a home, and this fifty grand could let me give him one.

What's the saying? The ends justify the means?

I open my mouth to answer JJ when there's a scuffling noise from inside JJ's bedroom. I muffle a giggle with my hand.

JJ, for her part, looks completely unashamed at having a man in there. "Well, if you're wavering at all on Maddox, I already have another date lined up for this weekend. Remember the guys you looked at on the app the other day? You thought that guy Zachary was a good option for a wedding date. You have a date with him tomorrow night, so let me know now if I should cancel."

I do remember that one from the app. He seemed like a good option to facilitate the winning of this bet.

For Julio. This amount of money would be life-changing for me, sure, but even more so for Julio. I can't turn my back on it without feeling like I'm failing him again.

"Go ahead. Set it up. I can't wait to meet Zachary." I do my best to muster enthusiasm.

JJ's finger hovers over her phone. "What about Maddox?"

"He's supposed to be in Las Vegas for a tournament this weekend."

She frowns. "Seriously, Holly? He goes out of town, and you go on a date with another guy?"

Okay, I'll admit it. This is not a good look. I

haven't even told JJ about the bet, have I? Maybe she'd understand.

"So... Maddox made me a bet a few weeks ago," I start.

Her eyebrow lifts.

"The deal is that if I bring a date to the wedding that I'm in love with, he'll give me fifty grand. If I lose, I'll agree to date him. And I'm doing that anyway, but just think of how far fifty thousand dollars would go for some of our foster kids. We could set up programs. I was even thinking I could get my own place and maybe apply to have Julio come live with me." The words come out in a rush.

JJ's eyebrow goes higher and higher as I talk, and by the time I finish, she's shaking her head. "This is the dumbest idea you've ever had, Holly. Your heart's in the right place, at least as far as the kids are concerned. But just think of what it'll do to Maddox. I'll set up this one, but that's it. And you have to tell him."

I bite my lip. "I'll come clean. I promise."

I'm supposed to meet Zachary at Salvatore's for dinner. My mind keeps circling back to the time

Maddox and I had dinner there, and each time, I do my best to shake the thought loose.

I'm wearing a dress of JJ's— one that actually holds my boobs in, thank fuck—and kitten heels. Zachary's profile didn't explicitly state how tall he was, so there's a good chance he's on the shorter side. I am too at five feet, three inches, so a shorter guy isn't a problem unless I show up in five-inch heels. Honestly, a shorter guy isn't a problem at all. He's not a real date. He's a means to an end, and if he seems cool, I'm going to lay all the cards out on the table tonight, be upfront with him.

We're meeting at the restaurant. The Uber drops me off at four minutes till seven, and I make my way inside. I don't see anyone who matches the profile picture. The hostess shows me to a table, where I busy myself with arranging my utensils while I wait.

Zachary shows up right on time. It's not quite meeting outside the venue and walking in together, but it's a hell of a lot better than my first date of this whole saga, who showed up so late that I started to wonder if I'd been stood up.

"Holly?" Zachary asks, holding a hand out in greeting.

I stand from my chair, noting that he's a good four or five inches taller than me, but not much more than that. Glad I skipped the five-inch heels. "Hi. Zachary? It's nice to meet you."

We shake hands, and he slides into the chair opposite me.

"So, Holly, tell me—"

The waitress chooses that moment to appear at our table, brandishing a list of specials. "Tonight, we have a salmon poached in butter and white wine…"

I only half listen as she drones on, but I'm grateful that she showed up when she did.

What was he going to say? *Tell me about yourself?* This is a date, not a job interview. Then again, the way I'm playing things, it kind of is a job interview.

We place our orders and hand the menus to the waitress, who walks away, leaving me alone with Zachary.

I pick up my water glass and bring it to my lips. "So, Zachary, what do you like to do?"

Yeah, it's a boring question, and not a great date question. But I'm hoping he'll ramble for a bit, and I won't have to talk about myself.

Sure enough, he takes the bait. "Well, I have a dog that I love to adventure with. His name is Oscar." Zachary pulls out his phone and swipes through things, then turns it around to show me a picture of a Saint Bernard. "He's my best friend. I've had him for about two years. Before that it was…" He swipes some more and shows me a picture of a dog that looks identical to the first. "Rosco. It was hard getting used to Oscar. He's just so different from Rosco."

"Mmm," I reply. What else does one say in this position? Those are two pictures of the same fucking dog. You're not going to convince me otherwise.

"What about you, Holly? Do you have any pets?"

I shake my head. "No, no pets."

Zachary's earnest look deflates. "Not even, like, a hamster?"

"There's the occasional rat in the basement of our apartment building, but other than that, no pets allowed."

He brightens. "That's something!"

That is not something. That is a pest control problem, not a pet. Would the cockroach I saw scuttling across the lobby the other day be *something* in the way of a pet as well?

I decide it's better not to bring it up. Based on his expression, I think he'd be personally offended and call PETA if I admitted that I sprayed Raid in all the corners of our place after I saw the roach. Better not bring that up. I need his cooperation here.

I try to change tactics. "I'm more into movies, TV,

that sort of thing. Books, too. My favorite is CSI, or maybe Law and Order."

"Oh! I love those shows. Anything crime related. And books on serial killers. Do you know much about Ted Bundy?" Zachary displays the same rabid enthusiasm toward serial killers as he does toward pets, which is mildly concerning.

Should I tell him serial killers usually start out as sociopaths who torture and kill animals before turning to humans?

"I can't say that I do."

Zachary launches into a soliloquy about Ted Bundy, which comes across as suspiciously admiring of the serial killer. I'm ready to give up on this guy, but I need his help.

Wedding date.

Fifty grand.

For Julio.

Focus, Holly.

"Here you are. One chicken piccata, one burger with fries. Would you like me to grab you some ketchup or other sauces for that?" The waitress sets my plate—chicken piccata—down with a flourish, then practically tosses Zachary's well-done burger in front of him.

"No thanks. I prefer my burger and fries plain." He gives her a beaming smile.

Plain?

I get that not everyone is as into my hot-sauce-and-mayo concoction. But most people would put *something* on their burger, or at least the fries. I smile to myself. Maddox would be drowning that sucker in ketchup.

Maddox.

I watch Zachary take another bite of his charred burger, seeing things even more clearly.

Zachary's not the one I want to sit here with. He's not the one I want to tell about my day and play board games with and cuddle in bed.

And as the realization dawns, I feel like I've been punched in the gut. Hard. JJ's right. She usually is, but typically not in a way that hits home so hard. Every minute I sit here is hurting Maddox. I owe him more than this.

My hangups about this whole wedding date thing came from a place of pain that's lingered for the last three years. I'm not going to solve it by hurting someone else.

I put my fork down. "I'm so sorry, Zachary. I enjoyed meeting you. But I need to leave." I stand up so suddenly that the napkin on my lap falls to the floor.

Zachary looks a bit stunned but not heartbroken, which is a relief, but only slightly.

I put some money on the table to cover my dinner as I slide my coat on. "I'm sorry," I say again.

How did it take five minutes to get here and it's taking five hours to get home? I need to get back to my place so I can call Maddox. I know he's at a tournament, so maybe he can't even talk, but I need to tell him everything. I need him to hear the whole story about my mom's funeral, no matter how much it hurts to talk about. I want to tell him about how I went out with Zachary tonight, and why, and hope like hell he can forgive me. I just hope it's not too late.

I practically run across the lobby when the rideshare drops me off at our building. The elevator takes longer than usual, too. I drum my fingers against my side impatiently.

My phone is in my hand when I put the key in the lock and push the apartment door open, but as soon as I do, I gape at the scene in front of me.

What's Maddox doing here?

20

MADDOX

I pulled out of the tournament in Vegas. Between Holly and a run of bad games, I think it's for the best, though. I'll do a smaller one in Atlantic City, maybe two, to make up for it.

Now I'm very glad I chose not to go, though.

When I rang the buzzer at the front door, another girl answered. The infamous JJ, Holly's roommate, who until now I've only seen from afar. She invited me up, and she's just delightful. Spunky, hilarious, and full of important information, like where Holly is and who she's with right now.

But more importantly, some information about exactly why. She didn't delve too deeply into it—like Robert, she understands that this is Holly's story to tell —but she shared enough for me to soften just a bit, and when she left for the evening, she let me stay here to wait for Holly.

I'm expecting it to be at least an hour, but I've only been sitting here for about twenty minutes when a key turns in the door.

Holly is holding her phone in her hand, her cheeks flushed with cold. Her mouth drops open when she sees me, and as I stand from the couch, her eyes fill with tears.

"I'm so fucking sorry, Maddox," she says, choking on the words. "I'm—"

The next words are muffled as I gather her in my arms and hold her tight against my chest as she sobs.

"I'm here, babe," I murmur against her hair. "I've got you."

If anything, this makes her cry even harder, but I just hold her until the tears dry up.

Finally, Holly draws in a shuddering breath and takes a step back. "There's a lot I need to tell you, Maddox. I feel like I fucked everything up."

I take her hand and we walk to the couch. Holly's gaze is fixed on her twisting fingers in her lap. I quietly wait for her to speak.

"I told you Jared cheated on me, and it was at my mom's funeral. With my cousin. Some of my relatives caught him, and everyone saw. It was such a painful time, losing my mom right around the holidays, but the thing that made it even worse was how my family treated me. Like him cheating was somehow my fault. I'd chosen the wrong guy, so what did I expect?"

The words keep pouring out, like all the emotion has been trapped inside her for so long. "And with the wedding, I knew I'd be seeing all those people again. The idea of them judging me for choosing the wrong guy again, my stepbrother of all people, just brought all those feelings back. The humiliation, but also the pain of losing my mom. It's why I was so desperate to find another date. One that was good on paper, that they'd approve of."

Holly takes a deep breath and looks up at me with watery, pleading eyes.

"I don't even know why the fuck I care. I don't even see them outside of major events like this. I haven't seen those relatives in three years. But I-I don't want another guy, Maddox. I don't know if I can face them at the wedding at all, but I don't want to bring a guy I don't love just for them.

"And then we made that bet, and somewhere along the line I started realizing just how much fifty thousand dollars is. How far it would go for my foster kids. How many programs I could fund with that. I even thought about getting my own place so I could take

Julio in myself. He's one of my favorite foster kids, the one I haven't found a place for yet. The one who might have to go to a group home."

My heart melts a little. Holly is the furthest thing from a gold digger. Most people would see fifty grand as a life-changing amount of money for themselves.

Holly sees it as life-changing for her foster kids.

She sniffles. "So I went on a date tonight. I thought if I found a guy that I could convince to go to the wedding with me, I'd win the bet. I was thinking about Julio, because he's all I've been focused on for work, and I feel like I'm failing him every day I can't find him a home. But now I've ruined everything. I'm so sorry, Maddox. I never meant to hurt you. I'm so, so sorry." A new set of tears courses down her cheeks.

I put my arm around her, and she leans into me, her tears soaking my t-shirt. "We're going to figure this out, Holly. I've got you."

When the tears dry up for a second time—or third? I'm losing track—I let her go and sit back on the remarkably uncomfortable couch.

"The ball has been in your court here since the beginning, Holly," I start. "You've known exactly where I stand, and I've followed your lead, but now it's my turn."

She blinks at me, nodding slightly. She looks

shocked that I haven't left, but like I keep telling her, I'm not going anywhere.

"I love your dedication to your foster kids. It means so much to me, you know that. But the money is off the table. I'm calling off the bet."

"But…"

I shake my head. "I'll put fifty grand toward foster programs in some capacity. But it's not going to depend on whether you bring a date to the wedding or anything like that."

She looks somewhat mollified by this.

"You don't need to bring a date to the wedding. You'll be surrounded by people who love you no matter what. You don't have to tell any relatives you're dating anyone. For that matter, you don't have to talk to them at all. Stick with Addie, and she'll do the talking."

That earns me a smile. A small one, but it's a start.

"And I wonder if you might consider talking to someone. About everything with your mom and what happened at the funeral. There's a lot to process there, and while I'm here for you, some of this you have to work through on your own. It's real trauma, Holly. It's not something you just muscle your way through."

I stop there and wait. Some people get defensive

when you lay it all out there, but Holly just looks deep in thought.

"I... I think you're right," she says softly, still focused on her lap. "I didn't think of it that way. All these kids I see daily have so much more going on in their lives that my problems seemed trivial in comparison, so I never thought about talking to a therapist or anything. Plus, I was busy taking care of my dad right after Mom died, and I pushed all my own feelings about everything away." She brings her gaze up to meet mine. "I'm going to find a therapist to talk to about everything after the holidays. But I'm so sorry I ruined everything, Maddox."

I put two fingers under her chin, keeping her gaze focused on me. "You didn't ruin things, Holly. I'm not going anywhere." I bring my lips to hers. I can taste the salt of her tears mixing with that signature sweet taste of her that I've come to love, and I say it again to make sure she hears me. "I'm not going anywhere. Now, grab your coat."

Holly pulls back from where our lips are still practically touching. "My coat?" Her eyes are dazed. A good emotional catharsis and making out will do that to you.

I nudge her off the couch. "The thing you wear when it's cold outside."

She gives my shoulder a playful shove as she picks up the jacket from where she dropped it in the entryway. I pull my own coat on and take her hand, leading her out of the apartment and into the cold air.

Holly shivers beneath the winter chill as we approach Rittenhouse Square Park.

The park is one of several in Philadelphia. This one sits close to the border between Center City—the main downtown—and University City, where I live and where several colleges are located. It's considered an upscale part of town, with its overpriced townhomes and luxury stores lining Walnut Street.

During the holiday season, the city hangs globes lined with twinkling lights from the lampposts and trees. They look like Christmas ornaments, and in the snow, it gives the darkened park a magical feeling. There's nothing quite like it.

"I forgot how beautiful it is here at Christmas," Holly breathes. She shivers again.

I pull off my coat and wrap it around her. I'm freezing my nuts off, and she looks like a snowman encased on both our jackets, but if she's warm, it's worth it. Plus, isn't this the scene from every Hallmark Christmas movie?

Holly smiles at me as she pulls the fleece tighter around her.

She's right. It *is* magic. The snow falling in mini, silent flakes. The peaceful feeling of the park when it's nearly empty. The twinkling lights. The Christmas tree in the very center of the walkway, lit up with what must be a million tiny lightbulbs.

It's romantic and magical and beautiful all at once. I tip my head back and stick my tongue out, catching a few flakes.

"Are you catching snowflakes on your tongue?" Holly asks, looking at me like I'm crazy.

"Yep," I say, sticking my tongue out again. "Try it."

Holly walks a few steps ahead of me, and I think she's going to ignore me. But when I look up, she's got her hands stretched out wide, her face turned up to the sky and her tongue out.

She's catching snowflakes, too.

She has a look of pure, innocent joy on her face, one I rarely see on adults. My breath catches in my throat. I want to remember this moment forever. I want to see her doing this with our kids one day.

"Maddox!" she calls, beckoning to me. "Come here!"

She holds out both of her hands to me. When I get close enough, she grabs both hands and twirls, spinning me in a circle right along with her.

When she stops, she collapses against me in dizzy giggles. I wrap my arms around her.

"Thank you," she says softly, tilting her head up toward me.

I tap her nose with my finger. It's pink with cold. I smile down at her. "Any time, babe."

She shakes her head just a bit. "I used to love Christmas. My mom went all out and always made it so special, even though it was just the three of us. She made it this big celebration, my birthday and Christmas all in one big day, and everything was so magical. Since she died, I haven't been able to enjoy the holidays. I haven't even really celebrated at all, because it reminded me of her, and it was just too much for me. But it was like the magic of Christmas died along with her."

She takes a deep breath. The unshed tears glisten in her eyes, reflecting the lights that hang everywhere. She blinks, and one traces a path down her cheek.

"Thank you for showing me the magic again."

21

HOLLY

I have one week left.

That's it.

One week to find Julio someplace to stay before he'll be stuck in a group home. And while Maddox and I are in a better spot, it doesn't put me any closer to finding a spot for Julio.

I poke my head into my supervisor's office. Adam Sanderson is constantly busy—we all are, it's a way of life at DHS—but his door is always open in case any of us needs anything. I knock on the doorframe.

"Hey, Holly, come in. What's going on?" Adam looks up from his computer and pulls his reading glasses off. His flannel shirt has a mustard stain on the front and his graying hair is pointed every which way, but his frazzled look is something I've come to love about him. Like he's more invested in the kids he helps than in his own appearance.

I take a few steps into the office. "Hey. I hate to ask for help, but…"

Adam puts out his hands. "That's what I'm here for. What do you need?"

Thank God for Adam. He's a little awkward, but he's a fabulous boss and always willing to help out.

"I have a long-term case that I'm trying to place in a new home. The current foster parents are done after the end of the year. I know it's crunch time, and with the holidays, I haven't been able to find a new home yet. I was hoping you had some magical solution."

Adam leans back in his chair and blows out a breath. "Hmm. I'm guessing you've spoken to all your contacts already?"

I nod. "Yep. No takers."

He brings his palms together and holds his hands in front of his mouth as he thinks. "How about other counties?"

"I was wondering about that option. Think that's my best bet?"

Adam sits upright and scribbles something on a piece of paper. "Here. Call Alexis at the regional office. She'll have contacts for all the different counties." He holds out the Post-it to me.

I take it and thank him while sending up a silent prayer. *Please, let someone have a spot for Julio.*

I make my way down the hall to my office. JJ is sitting at her desk, staring at her computer, but she whirls around when I walk in.

"Hey!" Her energy is back.

JJ is not a morning person. We rarely speak in the morning before coffee because she turns into a rabid beast and will claw you. Literally. Once, I asked if I could borrow her makeup brush while the coffee was still brewing.

She threw it at my head.

"Hey, JJ." I sink into my desk chair with a sigh.

"What's wrong?" Her brows pull together.

I spin my chair around to face her and slouch. "Still no place for Julio. I'm down to like a week. Technically, he can stay at Brad and Linda's until the thirty-first, but you know nothing will really get done between Christmas and New Year's unless it's an emergency placement." Tears well in my eyes. "He's going to end up in a group home."

JJ stands from her chair. She tugs me out of mine and pulls me into a hug. "Hey. It's going to be okay," she soothes. "You'll find him a place, even if he has to go to the group home for a little while. That's why we have them. And remember, this is what you do. It's not who you are." She pulls back, looking me in the eye. "First, this situation isn't a failure. And even if it were, a failure at work is not..."

"...a personal failure. I know." I roll my eyes. I'm not sure if I believe it this time.

"Right. You're a great social worker. You're a great *person*. And I know you love Julio, and he loves you too. And he'll still love you even if he has to spend some time in a group home. He's done it before, remember?"

I take a deep breath and nod. "You're right. Thank you." Her words do help, at least a little. "Adam gave me the number to one of the regional supervisors. I'm hoping she might give me a lead on other counties that might have openings."

"There you go. You've got this." JJ gives me another squeeze before releasing me and prancing over to her desk. "Now, gossip before or after you call them?"

I made JJ wait until lunch to gossip. We duck into our favorite sandwich shop, brushing off snow and pulling off mittens as soon as we're inside the cozy eatery. It's packed with people, some sitting at small tables and others squeezed close together on mismatched couches.

"It's really coming down now," JJ remarks, glancing outside. She pulls her hat off, letting her long curly hair spill down her back.

We order sandwiches—tuna for JJ, ham and Swiss for me—along with bowls of steaming soup and carry the food to an empty table by the window where we can watch the snow fall.

I unwrap my sandwich and hold it up. "Okay, JJ. Spill." I bite into the bread. It's loaded high with ham, with exactly the perfect amount of mustard.

She blows on her soup. "So. Um. Justin and me."

I tilt my head, waiting. "Yeah?"

JJ puts her spoon on the table and looks at me. "Are you okay with this? I mean, really okay? I know you went out with him first, and I know you kind of liked him."

I think for a minute. I did like him, but it was just that. I liked him. I enjoyed hanging out with him. After all, he was basically the male version of me.

No wonder JJ likes him. I snicker to myself.

"What?" JJ narrows her eyes at me.

Oops. She wasn't supposed to hear that, but JJ and I don't keep secrets. "I was just thinking that you like him because he's the male version of me."

JJ stares at me for a minute, then bursts into laughter. Then I laugh, and soon we're both giggling so hard that tears are running down our faces.

JJ wipes her face with the back of her hand. "God, I love you so much."

"Love you too, girl. So are you in love with man-me?" I tease.

But JJ isn't laughing anymore.

"JJ?"

She looks at her lap, then back at me. "I, um... I think I am."

Holy shit. "Wow. That happened fast."

JJ shrugs, her cheeks flaming.

"I mean, I haven't said it to him or anything," she explains. "And I don't know where it's going. But yeah. I think this is the real deal, Holly. And I want to know that you're okay with it. You know I'd never steal a guy from you, and I know you were okay with me going out with him, but this... this is bigger. And I feel like I need your blessing again before we keep going down this path."

Now it's my turn to pull JJ out of her seat and wrap her in a hug. "Of course, girl. He's perfect for you. I can see how happy you are." And I can. She's practically glowing. "And maybe one of these days we can double date."

We sit back in our seats, and JJ picks up her sandwich.

She says, "While I'm blissfully maybe in love and happy to talk about it nonstop, I think I need to hear about your life, too. I let a very nice gentleman into our apartment the other day who was there looking for you. I haven't heard how that turned out." JJ gives me a pointed look.

There's silence.

Where do I start?

"I left the date with Zachary early," I say hesitantly.

She nods, eating. "Probably good."

"And Maddox was in our apartment when I got back."

JJ nods again, moving her sandwich in front of her in a circle as tuna salad threatens to spill out from the sides. "Go on."

"And I... told him everything. All the stuff from the incident, how it's still buried deep. Why I even went out with the weird dry burger guy."

JJ looks perplexed.

"Zachary. He eats his hamburger with no ketchup."

"Ew. Red flag." JJ takes a bite, cringing.

I chuckle. "It was almost... fate, maybe, if that's a thing. Maddox loves ketchup. He puts it on everything. And when Zachary didn't, it made me realize more than ever that I wanted to be there with Maddox. How much I was hurting him. I was a bitch to him, JJ. I was awful."

She shrugs. "I kind of tried to tell you."

True. "I know, and I owe you an apology too, 'cause I didn't listen."

"Forgiven," she says easily. "But now what's happening with this bet you made? It was kind of stupid to gamble with feelings, you know."

You don't have to tell me that.

"We... Maddox called it off. He said he'll figure out a way to donate to the foster program, if that's what I want, but the bet is over." I pick at my sandwich. It feels kind of anticlimactic, in a way. I got the guy, but I still haven't fixed the problem with finding a place for Julio.

"Good," JJ says, pleased. "So, then you banged?"

"JJ! We did not bang. I mean, not right then, anyway." My cheeks flush. "We went for a walk. He took me through Rittenhouse, actually. It's all lit up for Christmas. You know how they decorate with the lights all over the trees? I haven't seen it at night like this in a couple years. Everything felt so magical. It just..." I stop, unable to get the words past the lump in my throat.

JJ waits until I can keep going.

I swallow. "It was magical," I say again. "It felt the way Christmas used to feel. When my mom was alive. And..."

This time there's no stopping the silent tears that start to fall.

It wasn't the walk through the park.

The beauty of the lights strung up in Rittenhouse touched something inside me, but I don't think that's what's caused this feeling. I think it was the person I was with. Because since Maddox and I walked together through the lit-up Christmas wonderland of the park, I've had this feeling inside me that I only remember feeling during the holidays.

A warmth surrounding me, shielding me from the icy winter air.

Lightness, happiness. Anticipation.

A feeling of comfort, like no matter what happens in the year ahead, it'll be okay because we're together.

I'm going with Judy to pick up my dress for the wedding. She insisted on seeing me try it on but promised me lunch after the fitting.

She's the least bridezilla I've ever seen this close to a wedding, so I'll give her this one.

I pull on the gown in the dressing room. It's a perfect fit, and the color is flattering on me. It's knee-length, so it's definitely something I'll wear again. I smooth out the skirt and spin in front of the mirror.

"How does it look?" Judy calls from outside the dressing room. "Come show me!"

It feels like I've known Judy much longer than the few weeks I have. I can see how my dad fell in love with her so quickly. Her calm, unassuming demeanor puts you at ease. She's easy to talk to.

Except about her son, but we'll get there.

When I step out of the fitting room, Judy brings her hands to her mouth. "Oh, you look beautiful, Holly," she says.

I do another twirl in front of the mirror. I feel pretty. The light purple color suits me.

Something occurs to me, though. "Judy, how come you chose purple for a Christmas Eve wedding? It doesn't seem like a very Christmassy color."

"Well..." She tilts her head. "I wasn't sure if you'd be okay with us launching into the Christmas theme. I know that was a very special time for you and your mother. I don't want to overstep. And this wedding is for fun. I don't need a fancy wedding, and I don't care about colors or themes. All I care about is marrying Robert and sharing our happiness with all of you."

I don't cry. Okay, I rarely cry. But somehow over the last several weeks I've turned into a full-on fountain of tears. The fact that Judy took my feelings into consideration when planning her *wedding*?

Tears prick at my eyes. "Judy, that's so kind of you. Thank you for thinking of me." I smile as one tear escapes and makes its way down my cheek. "But I think I'm okay now, or getting there. I'm ready to celebrate Christmas again. To make new memories."

Maybe that's what the tears are. All the feelings and memories I've shoved so far down inside me are making their way to the surface and spilling out.

Judy holds her arms out. "Oh, Holly. I love you already, sweetheart. I can't wait to make memories with you."

MADDOX

I drum my fingers on the counter, waiting. I was supposed to pick up my tux for this wedding a few days ago. The supposedly *small* wedding.

I should have known better. Mom loves to plan events. Somehow, she's managed to turn this from friends-and-family-only to a massive, invite-everyone-we-know affair. And despite the fact that the wedding is happening on Christmas Eve, and that she organized and planned the whole thing in a month's time, about a zillion people have said yes.

Well, sixty. But that's a lot when you consider that they originally said this was going to be less than fifteen people.

And now there are matching dresses for my sisters and Holly, and I'm renting a tux.

"Ah! Here we are." Mario appears from the back of the store. His wiry grey hair and glasses perched at the end of his nose make him look like a little old man who was born and raised in Italy, and he was, with the hand gestures and the accent to prove it.

I slide my credit card across the counter as Mario hands me the tux. "Thanks, Mario. Appreciate it."

He runs my card and hands it back. "Anytime, son. You have friends who need a suit, you tell them to come see Mario, eh?"

She looks stunning.

For the rehearsal dinner, Holly is wearing a dark blue dress that just skims her knees. Her arms are bare, and the front of the dress dips down just a little in the front between her tits, giving her the classiest and hottest hint of cleavage ever. The outline of the dress dips in at her waist and flares out at the skirt, making her curves look even more lush.

I'm sure there's a name for the style, but who the fuck cares? I just hope the dress she's wearing tomorrow is similar.

Unlike the wedding, which has grown in scope considerably, the rehearsal dinner really is just friends and family, and no dates are necessary. The decorations lean into the Christmas theme, including a pine tree strung with lights and laden with ornaments, wreaths, and mistletoe strategically hung. There are only four small tables, each seating four people.

This is my kind of party.

I make my way to the bar and order a lager. The bartender uncaps the bottle and slides it toward me. As I take a long sip, I look for Holly.

She's engaged in a conversation with Addie, but her gaze locks on mine. She smiles shyly.

I smile back and crook a finger, then order her a vodka cranberry while she walks toward me.

"You look amazing," I greet her, handing her the drink.

She takes the glass from me, blushing slightly. "Thanks. This is JJ's dress. As usual."

"Well, you should steal it from her. That was made for you." I hold my bottle out. "Cheers. It's good to see you, Holly."

She clinks her glass against my bottle, and we each bring our drink to our mouths.

Holly fiddles with her glass silently.

I bump her playfully with my hip. "Really, it's good to see you. I know it's been a couple weeks since I saw you last. I'm hoping the magic of Christmas hasn't worn off just yet."

Her cheeks color slightly, but she's smiling. "No. Not yet. Thank you for the text messages each day." She hesitates.

I fill the silence. "You're welcome." I wink. "Plus, I wanted to give you time to miss me."

She smiles and lifts her glass to her lips. "Maybe I did."

Addie insisted on a girls' table for dinner, and for reasons that remain unclear to me, Judy went along with it. So now I'm sitting at a table with Robert, my sister-in-law Chris who flat out refused to join the girls' table with "all their gossip," as she put it, and my Uncle Steve. And I'm staring across the room at Holly. She has her head thrown back, laughing at something one of my sisters said.

Maybe I should have involved myself in the planning a bit. Then I'd be sitting next to her instead of hearing about Uncle Steve's knee replacement.

"Maddox, will you be coming for Christmas? We'll have dinner on Christmas Day before we leave on our honeymoon." Robert's voice breaks through my reverie.

I force my attention back to our table. "Sure. At your house or my mom's?"

Robert takes a sip of his beer and puts the glass on the table. "I'm moving into your mom's house. I more or less live there already, and it makes sense. There's more space, extra bedrooms. We'll put my old place on the market in January."

"Makes sense," I say. "I'm going to hit the men's room, then grab a drink at the bar. Would anyone like anything?"

By the time I make it to the bar, everyone has finished dinner. People are milling around, socializing. I look for Holly, but I don't see her. I order another lager.

I carry it while I make small talk, keeping my eyes peeled for Holly. Where *is* she?

By the time I make it to my mother, I still haven't seen Holly. It's been at least twenty minutes since I came back from the restroom. Should I be worried?

"Hi, Mom. Beautiful dinner." I give her a hug. "Are you enjoying yourself?"

"Oh, of course. I can't wait for tomorrow. It will

be so beautiful. Do you like the Christmas theme?" She gestures around, like I haven't been surrounded by the decorations for the last two hours.

"I love it, Mom. I'd expect nothing less from a Christmas lover like you. I'll bet Holly likes it, too. She loves Christmas." She and my mom have a lot in common, actually. I can picture them becoming great friends. "Actually, have you seen her?"

A hint of a smile tugs at my mom's lips. "She's here, of course. Why?"

I shrug, going for nonchalant. "Just curious. I saw her earlier, but I haven't seen her in a bit. Wondering if she left already."

Mom's eyes sharpen as she looks around the room. "Let me check the ladies' room."

I pull out my phone and call Holly while she checks, but it goes to voicemail.

She returns a few minutes later. "She's not in there. Did you call her?"

I nod. "No answer."

Mom is starting to look frantic. Fuck, I don't want to ruin her rehearsal dinner, but I'm getting worried too.

"Robert?" she calls, motioning to Holly's dad. "We can't find Holly. Have you seen her?"

He does the same thing my mom did, looking

around, as though Holly might be in this small room and both of us somehow missed her. "Huh. No, I haven't. I was talking to her a bit ago. She was going to the ladies' room, but I haven't seen her since."

"She's not in there now." My mom wrings her hands.

Wait.

I look at Robert. "Did you talk to her about moving in with my mom? About selling your house?"

He nods. "Yeah, I did. Why?"

I'm already grabbing my jacket from the coat rack and sliding my arms into the sleeves. "I know where she is."

"Holly?"

The weathered colonial frame is only lit by the reflection of the moon in the snow. Most of the windows are dark, but when I pull into the driveway, there's one upstairs window lit. She's here. I know it.

I close the front door behind me and turn on a light. There's a set of stairs just to my right. The upstairs hallway is dark, but a bit of light spills out from one room just beyond the top of the staircase.

"Holly, I'm coming up there."

There's no answer. The walls along the staircase are lined with framed photographs, just like my mom's house. There's one of a couple. The man looks like a younger Robert. Hell, it probably is. There's a dark-haired woman with her arms around him, a smile stretched wide across her face. Holly's mother.

I take a few more steps. There's one of an infant that must be Holly, of a young Holly with her mother holding flowers, the two of them beaming into the camera.

There's so much love in this house. I can understand why Holly is heartbroken at the idea of losing it.

The floor creaks at the top of the stairs. "Holly?" I call out again.

The door just to the right of the staircase is slightly open, light coming from within. I push it open gently.

Holly is curled up on a twin bed, fast asleep. Her eyes are red-rimmed from crying. Her body rises and falls softly with her slow, steady breathing.

I sit on the edge of the bed and smooth her hair back. "Holly," I whisper. "It's me. It's Maddox."

She stirs but doesn't open her eyes. "Maddox?"

"Yeah, babe. It's me. I'm here. Wake up."

She blinks, then rubs her hand across her eyes. "What time is it?"

I smile. "It's eight o'clock. You've been here for less

than an hour, but you fell asleep. You okay?"

She licks her lower lip and slowly sits up. "Um. I don't know."

I shift, putting my arm around her shoulders. "Your dad told you he was selling the house, huh? Moving in with my mom?"

She nods. Tears glisten in her eyes again.

"That must be really tough."

She nods again, and a tear spills out. "This was just always home, you know? I feel like..."

She trails off, and I wait silently.

Holly draws in a shaky breath. "Maybe it's silly. But I kind of feel like my mom is still here, somehow. And if we sell the house, it's like I'm losing her all over again."

She dissolves in tears, and I wrap my other arm around her, holding her close. I rub her back while she sobs. It's several minutes before she pulls back, rubbing her eyes.

Holly murmurs, "I'm sorry. I don't know why I'm so sentimental."

"Nothing to be sorry for. I get it, I really do. We're going to figure out how to fix this, okay?"

"Okay." She sniffles.

"Now, show me around this house. I want to hear all about your memories of growing up here."

❄

We walk around the two-story home, with Holly pointing out her favorite features and sharing memories. It's a beautiful house, with stained glass in the front door and a secret room between the hallway and the guest room on the first floor.

Holly is giggling as she steps into the small area. "Come on in! It's small, but this is one of my favorite places in this house."

I duck my head to step through the opening, turning sideways so my shoulders will fit. There's not much light in here, but what filters in from the hallway illuminates a bookshelf.

"This was always my reading area. You could probably tell from all the books." She gives a little shrug, but she's smiling. "There used to be a light in here."

"What were your favorites?" I ask, stepping toward the bookshelf. It's lined with mystery novels, everything from the Hardy Boys to James Patterson.

The true crime addiction makes more sense now.

"This one." Holly pulls a book off the shelf. "It's a classic. From what I can remember, this was the first mystery book my mom ever bought me. And..." She spreads her arms as wide as she can in the small space. "I was hooked."

She holds the book out to me, and I take it. It's a hardback, the pages yellowed with age. I read the title out loud. "Nancy Drew and the Secret of the Old Clock."

Holly nods. "It's the very first Nancy Drew book. Have you ever read them?"

I haven't. "I've read the Hardy Boys, but not Nancy Drew. Should I read this?"

"Absolutely. Take that copy. Let me know what you think."

I turn it over in my hands. It's in good shape, but fragile. "This one seems pretty old, Holly. I don't want to ruin it." I flip it open to check when this one was published, but it's too dark in this room to see.

I step into the hallway for better light and open the book to the first page, Holly standing next to me.

There's a name inside the front cover. "Who's Marcy Monroe?" I ask.

Holly reaches out to take the book from me. "That was my mom's maiden name." She runs her finger over it. "This was her set from when she was a kid. I'd forgotten." She raises her eyes and looks around at the hallway wistfully, taking in the rooms we can see from where we are. "There's just so much of her here. I can't let him sell this place."

23

───────

HOLLY

'm feeling so guilty as Maddox drives us back to the hotel where the rehearsal dinner is being held. At this point, the dinner is probably over. I hate that I ruined this for my dad and Judy.

When Dad mentioned off-handedly that he was planning to sell the house, something snapped inside me. I can't explain it, even now. I just knew I needed to get to the house and be close to Mom. It felt like it might be my last chance. Everything is changing so quickly, and I need it all to slow down.

I lean my head against Maddox's shoulder. "How did you know where to find me?"

He brushes a kiss over my forehead. "I know you, babe. Better than you think. When your dad told me

285

he'd mentioned selling the house, I knew you'd gone there. I just asked him for a key and the address."

There's no one left when Maddox and I finally make it back to the dinner. We look around the space, where a cleaning crew is wiping down tables.

"Crap. I guess I missed it." Guilt settles heavily in my stomach. I didn't mean to ruin their rehearsal dinner. At least we'd eaten before I left, but I missed the toasts. I'd wanted to say something about my dad, about how lucky the two of us are to have Judy in our lives.

Maddox looks at his phone. "It sounds like everyone just headed back home." He raises his eyes to me. "Do you want a ride?"

I know the wedding is tomorrow, and I'll need most of the day to get ready. I know I need a good night's sleep. And I know this isn't what good girls do. But I don't care.

I shake my head. "I want to get a room."

Maddox looks at me quizzically.

"With you," I clarify. I lock my gaze on his and watch his pupils dilate.

Maddox pulls on the back of his neck. "Are you sure this is what you want, babe? I know it's been an emotional day. And I know the last time we—" He breaks off, scratching at his hair. "Fuck, Holly. I don't want you to think I'm taking advantage of you. I don't want to do that to you, and I don't think I can go through that again."

I cringe slightly. He's right. The last time we were together was after Jared showed up at my apartment. It was hot and heavy, driven by lust and the need to chase Jared out of my head. But this is different.

This time, I'm not coming to him for comfort, needing a friend. This time, I know exactly what I asking for.

"I'm sure. Please," I whisper.

There's an older couple in the elevator with us. They're adorable, the woman with gray, curled hair and a hunched back, and the man with a comb-over and stirrups holding his pants up. They're holding hands and making eyes at one another. I could describe them in even more detail if you want, because I've been staring at them since the second they got onto the elevator right before the door closed.

Because if I look at Maddox, I'm going to jump his bones. And I don't want to be responsible for Fred and Ethel here having a heart attack.

The elevator comes to a stop as we reach the tenth

floor and they hobble off, so slowly that Maddox has to hold the door open before it closes on them. We stand next to each other silently, watching the doors slide closed.

And the second they do, we're all over one another. Maddox fists his hand in my hair and crushes his lips on mine. I grip his shirt, struggling to stay upright as my knees buckle. He nips my lower lip, and I moan into his mouth.

We're breathing heavily when the doors open again on the twelfth floor. Maddox takes my hand and leads me down the hallway.

I barely take in the room. Once the door closes, Maddox locks it, and we pick up where we left off in the elevator. He presses me up against a wall and kisses me, his lips hard against mine. His tongue dips inside my mouth. His smell surrounds me; it's all man, rugged and strong. His hand cups my breast and squeezes gently.

Maddox's beard brushes my cheek as his low voice speaks in my ear. "Take your dress off, baby."

The butterflies rise in my stomach as I turn around and pull my hair to the side so he can undo the zipper. He drags it down, letting the dress fall off my shoulders then down to my waist before dropping completely to the floor in a puddle of blue satin.

Maddox kisses my bare shoulder. He moves the strap of my bra to the side, then does the same thing on the other side. He undoes the clasp before he spins me around while the undergarment slips down my arms and joins the dress on the floor.

He steps back and drags his gaze down my body. I squirm, vulnerable under the weight of his stare.

Maddox drags his hand over his chin. "Fuck, Holly. You're so fucking gorgeous."

I bite my lip as my face heats. I don't have to worry about responding, though, because Maddox presses his lips against mine. His hands move down my arms from my shoulders, then to my hips before he skims them up my sides until his thumbs barely touch the underside of my breast.

"Gorgeous," he says again, as he takes a step back to stare at my chest. He rubs his thumbs over my nipples.

I let out a low moan as the sensation goes straight to my core. Maddox responds by lowering his head and sucking one nipple into his mouth.

Holy Jesus fuck. Is it possible to come from nipple play alone?

I'm getting close when he switches to the other side and uses two fingers to pinch the one he left behind. The combination of pain and pleasure is almost too much, but when he frees my nipples, I need more.

Maddox takes a step back while I lean against the wall, panting. He pulls his shirt up and over his head, then sheds his pants, standing before me clad only in his boxers. He pulls those down too, freeing his large erection. He tugs my underwear down, going slowly until they're just above my knees. He lets them fall to the ground, then gathers me in a tight embrace.

His hard body presses against mine, his length firm against my stomach.

Maddox speaks in my ear, low and dark, "Are you sure, Holly?"

"Yes. I want this." I've never been more certain of anything in my life.

He picks me up, holding my knees on either side of him while the wall keeps me upright.

"Someday, I'm going to fuck you up against a wall just like this, baby," he says.

My heart beats faster.

My breath hitches in my chest.

My pussy clenches.

"But tonight, I want you in the bed. Hold onto my shoulders."

He steps back, holding me as I wrap my arms

around his neck. He carries me to the bed and sets me gently down.

Maddox reaches into the pocket of his discarded pants and pulls out a foil packet.

"You brought a condom to the rehearsal dinner?" I ask.

Maddox shrugs as he rips the foil and rolls the condom down his length in one smooth movement. "I was being optimistic. Now, get your ass further onto that bed and spread your legs."

I smirk, but I move into the center of the bed. Maddox climbs onto the mattress and settles between my legs. His cock notches at my entrance. My smirk fades as I bite my lip.

"Maddox," I whisper.

He stares into my eyes as he thrusts forward, burying himself inside me. I arch into him as he starts to move.

The sensations build within me. This is brand-new.

I've had sex with Maddox before. But this time, he's not a one-night stand. He's not a friend who took pity on me.

He's the man I love.

Fuck, I love him.

My eyes start to tear up with the overwhelming

emotions that are mingling with the pleasure building inside me.

Maddox slows. "Baby. Are you okay?"

I nod. "I'm more than okay." I move my pelvis against him. "More. I need more."

He pulls out of me completely and climbs off the bed. I let out a whimper, but before the sound is entirely out of my mouth, Maddox grips my ankles and pulls me to the side of the bed.

My ass is at the edge, and I'd fall off if it weren't for Maddox holding my legs up. He moves me so my ankles rest on his shoulders, then positions his cock at my entrance again.

"You need more, baby?" A smile plays at his lips.

I nod, letting out a whine. I need to feel him inside me. I need that connection.

He drives inside me, hard, and at this angle he goes deeper, hitting that spot inside me that has me seeing stars.

"Fuck!" I gasp.

Maddox keeps going, thrusting hard and fast, and all I can do is hold on. I'm about to come, just on the edge, when he slows down, trading speed for force.

"I'm going to come, baby. Are you close?"

I nod. "I'm there."

He increases the speed of his thrusts again and

brings his hand between us. He presses on my clit, and I tighten around him. As my climax wracks my body, I feel him stiffen, then jerk inside me with his own release.

"Good morning, beautiful," Maddox says, leaning over to nuzzle my hair.

"Mmm. Good morning." I give him a sleepy smile. Just like last night, everything about this is different. It's not awkward, the way it usually is to wake up next to someone. It feels right. Normal. I want to wake up like this every day. "What time is it?"

Maddox reaches over and checks the time on his phone. "Ten thirty." He moves back toward me. "Want to—"

"Ten *thirty*?" I shriek. "Fuck. I have to go home and get my dress. I have to do my hair, and my makeup, and be at the wedding by four. I'll never make it." I throw the covers off me, the duvet narrowly missing Maddox's head.

"Jesus, fuck!" he yelps. "Slow your roll, woman. I'll drive you home, but I can't drive if I'm blind from being pelted in the eye by a blanket."

I'm halfway to the bathroom already, my stress

levels rising. "This is going to be a disaster. It's going to take forever to get into the city. We're out on the Main Line, remember? Crap, crap, crap."

I'm hyperventilating over the sink when Maddox's hands press on my shoulders and spin me around.

"Holly. It will be fine. Take a breath."

I follow him as he breathes in, holds it, then breathes out.

"Good. Again."

We repeat the cycle five times, and it actually helps. By the time I blow out the last big breath, my heart has slowed somewhat.

I'm still going to be fucking stressed all day, though.

He tips my face up with two of his fingers under my chin. "This is a happy day, remember? You could show up to that wedding wearing ripped jeans and they'd just be happy you're there. We're not going to stress. We can keep our relationship to ourselves and tell people after. There's no reason to involve your relatives that, from what I can tell, are not nice people. Okay?"

I take another deep breath and nod when he releases my chin.

"Now, put some clothes on and I'll drive you

home. And it's Christmas Eve," he points out, his logic calming. "There's not much traffic right now."

Thank God for JJ.

As soon as I walked into the apartment in last night's wrinkled dress, she jumped into action, ready to help with makeup and hair while I filled her in on last night's events.

"More details. Does he talk dirty? How is he with his hands?"

I close my eyes and smirk, doing my best to hold still as she lines my eyes with liquid liner. "He knows what to say. And as far as his hands... let's just say I'm very happy."

JJ squeals as she moves to the other eye.

I know Maddox is right, that my dad and Judy wouldn't care what I look like, but it's not just them I want to look good for. I want to see that look on Maddox's face again. When his jaw drops slightly and his eyes widen, and it's all because of me.

"Are you staying at the hotel tonight?" JJ asks, moving on to the mascara.

I almost shrug and stop myself at the last minute. I don't want to smear the makeup that JJ has so painstakingly done while my hair sets in hot rollers. "I… maybe? Maddox and I are going to spend the night together, but I didn't get a chance to ask him if we were going to his place or staying at the hotel tonight. I was in too much of a hurry this morning."

Because we slept in after staying up fucking half the night. But I want him again.

"Okay, open," JJ says, finished with mascara. She has a smirk on her face that says she knows exactly why we were running late. She hands me a tube of lipstick. "Here. Do your lips while I take the rollers out. You're going to knock his socks off. And maybe his pants, too. If you're lucky."

24

HOLLY

After much debate on the merits of driving versus just taking an Uber, I settle on driving myself to the wedding. Maddox was right about there not being much traffic, but the snow is starting to come down, and I wish for the three millionth time that I drove a car with four-wheel drive.

I probably should have asked Maddox for a ride again. He drives a Subaru STI. It's a sporty little car that looks fast but also has all-wheel drive, and it would certainly be better in snow than this one with its tires that are a year past needing to be replaced. I tap my brakes again. It's also hard to drive in heels, especially when your toes are frozen.

But my dress for today is still fabulous. I felt like a princess putting it on.

I pause at a stoplight and sneak a peek down at the dress, where the skirt comes out from underneath my huge puffy coat. I hope everything goes well today. It's supposed to be a simple ceremony, short and sweet.

I haven't talked to my dad since last night. I cross my fingers that I can get there in time to talk with him before everything gets crazy. I know he didn't mean to upset me, and it makes sense that he and Judy would move in together now that they're getting married. It just hadn't dawned on me before then what that meant for the house, and I wasn't ready to hear it. I'm still not really ready to process it, if I'm being honest. But that's life, right? Things change, for better or worse, and we move on as best we can.

I squint through the falling snow, trying to keep the car on the road. The snow is really coming down.

"Turn left at the next light," my GPS instructs.

I do my best to focus on driving safely in the snow while also trying to get there on time, but what I really want to think about is Maddox. I'm in love with him. Is it too fast? Is it too soon to say it?

And how in the world are we going to hide our relationship today, when all I want to do is be with him all the time?

I feel like I'd be nervous on my wedding day. How do you know if you're making the right choice? What if your betrothed changes their mind at the last minute? How do you calm those wedding day jitters?

But my dad isn't nervous in the least. He and Judy each have an area where they're gathering before the ceremony, separate from one another. He's in a tux, kicked back on the sofa and watching an Eagles game.

I push his feet off the sofa and onto the floor, taking a seat on the couch next to him. "Hey, Dad. Congratulations."

He gives me a side hug with one arm, then flashes me his trademark grin as he pulls back. "Hey, Holly. Was worried about you last night."

"I wanted to apologize. I shouldn't have run off like that. It makes sense that you're going to move in with Judy. And I support it, of course. It just surprised me. That's all."

My dad waves me off. "Water under the bridge. I just want to make sure you're okay. Did you at least get dessert before you left?"

I nod. I didn't get dessert, but I'm okay. More than okay, in fact. "Thanks... thanks for sending Maddox to get me. I appreciate it."

My dad's brows knit together. "I didn't send him, sweetheart. He's the one who knew where you were.

All I did was give him the address." He tilts his head, looking into my eyes. "He's a good man, you know. You should give him a chance."

"I..." I'm not really sure what to say here. Does he know that Maddox and I have something going on?

A knock on the door saves me from having to ask.

Josie pops her head in the room. "Holly? Robert? It's time for the ceremony."

Dad and I stand up. He holds his arms open to me, then wraps me in a tight hug. "I'm so proud of you, Holly."

My face is smooshed against him, but I manage to get a few words out. "I'm happy for you, Dad. Mom would be glad to see you so happy."

He gives me a tighter squeeze. "Thanks, peanut. That means a lot."

The ceremony is short and sweet, just as planned. The guests sit in rows of chairs, and we stand up in front of them—my dad, me, Josie, and Addison.

Judy walks down the short aisle on Maddox's arm. He flashes me a wink as he hands his mom to my dad and moves to stand on my dad's other side.

I try to listen as they say their vows, but my mind is on Maddox.

I look over at him again. He makes eye contact, and his lips twitch with a smile.

Hiding this is going to be torture.

The hour after the ceremony is a flurry of pictures, cocktail hour, and changing into some shoes that I can actually walk in. I sigh with relief when I slip off the pumps and slide my feet into ballet slippers.

Now in my flats, I make my way back to the hotel ballroom. People are still milling around, but a few are starting to take their seats. The bar is set up in one corner of the room, the wines that Robert and Judy selected lined up on the bar. There should be enough time to grab a drink at the bar before dinner, right? I glance over at my assigned table. Finding it empty, I make my way to the bar.

"What can I get for you, love?" The bartender puts down the glass he's wiping dry as I walk up.

"A white wine, please." They're serving a buffet, which I happen to know includes both fish and chicken. Plus, I like white wine. Yes, even with steak.

He turns to get the bottle, and a blonde woman joins me at the bar. She doesn't look familiar, but then again, I don't know most of Judy's family or friends.

I turn to her, trying to be social, or at least polite.

"Hi. I'm Holly, Robert's daughter. Are you a friend of Judy's?"

She flashes me a smile. Her straight white teeth stand out against tanned skin. She chould be in a toothpaste commercial. "Hi there. I'm Ashley. I—"

The bartender sets a wineglass on the bar in front of me, then uncorks a bottle and pours a glass of chardonnay. "Here you go. Enjoy the party." He turns to Ashley.

"I'll take a white wine as well, thanks." She looks back at me while the bartender grabs another glass. "And yes, I know Judy. She's my mother-in-law."

I pick up my glass of wine and take a sip. It's cold and crisp, with buttery undertones. "Mother-in-law. So you're married to..." I'm thinking. Josie is married to Chris. Addison is single, as far as I know. Do they have another sibling?

"Maddox," she says, and my heart drops all the way to the ballet slippers I changed into for the reception.

I feel gutted. My heart pounds in my chest. *This can't be happening again.*

Ashley laughs, reminding me that she's still standing in front of me. "You look surprised."

Maddox wouldn't lie to me like this, I know he wouldn't, but this is too close to *The Incident*. I need to get away. "I, uh, just didn't know he was married. But I only met him recently." Both true statements. "Can you excuse me? I'm going to find my table. It was nice meeting you."

I step away from the bar, looking around again. I see Maddox across the room, engaged in conversation with some people I haven't met. I take a few steps toward him, then stop, reconsidering.

If I go to him now, everyone will know. Everyone will see Holly being made a fool of once again. Better to get away from all of this before I give them fodder for their gossip.

My hands are tingling, and my breath is coming in short gasps.

I need to get out of here.

The snow is falling pretty hard outside, which is going to make it tough to get home in my car. I have had two drinks, though, so maybe it's for the best that I don't drive right now. I wonder how much it would cost to get a room here?

I take the elevator to the second floor and find my room a few doors down the hall. The bathroom light is the only thing illuminating the room when I enter, but that's enough for me. I'd rather have my pity party in the dark, anyway.

I toss my purse on the dresser, kick off my flats, and flop down on the bed.

I lay there motionless for a few minutes before grabbing one of the pillows and holding it over my face as I scream my frustration into it.

Once the dam breaks, everything flows out in hot tears of emotion. I thought all those bottled-up emotions were done making me cry, but turns out there are more. Every bit of pain, grief, and self-doubt pours out of me. I scream into the pillow over and over, letting it all spill out.

The anger at myself for failing to find Julio a foster home.

The sadness that he'll have to go to a group home.

Fury at the grip Jared and his betrayal still have on me.

Frustration at myself for not being strong enough to move past what happened at Mom's funeral. Guilt for ruining Dad and Judy's wedding on top of every-thing at the rehearsal dinner.

And above all, the pain of my heart breaking. Because despite everything, the family and warmth I thought was growing around me these last weeks, I'm alone.

25

MADDOX

What the fuck is Ashley doing here?

I thought I was rid of the manipulative gold-digger a few years ago.

She and I were dating back when my dad got sick and when he died. I'd thought she was my angel, standing by me while he went into hospice. She held my hand at his funeral. We married a few months before he died, so he could be there. Ashley's idea.

Then as soon as the life insurance money was available, she had an agenda. And it was all about the money. Looking back, I should have known. She was always obsessed with status. She had to have the most expensive haircut, the top-of-the-line purse, the insanely high-priced shoes, spray tans, teeth whitening.

She wasn't my type, not anywhere close. But I was

emotionally vulnerable after Dad died. We all were. That's when Josie married Chris too, although hers seems to have worked out.

We weren't all so lucky.

Ashley is the reason I haven't wanted to pursue a relationship for years, never wanting more than one night with any girl. Until Holly.

I tug on the back of my neck. I don't see Holly anywhere. The last time I caught a glimpse of her, she was at the bar, which is where Ashley is now. From there, it's not that hard to put two and two together.

I may not use my undergrad psych degree, but I remember a few things.

If Ashley said something to Holly, she could have triggered a trauma response. Holly needs me.

I know I said I'd give her space today, pretend we weren't together for one more day, but I can't let her be alone if she's going through something.

With a glance out the window, I can see that the snow is starting to pile up. She must be somewhere in the hotel still.

I find Addie standing with Josie and Chris at the bar on the other side of the room, away from Ashley, deep in conversation with Cam. They all turn to smile at me as I walk up.

"Have you guys seen Holly?" I ask with no preamble.

They exchange a confused look.

"No. Why?" Addie brings her drink to her lips.

I pull my hand through my hair. "Because Ashley is here. And I think she might have said something to Holly. I don't know what, but now Holly isn't answering my calls."

They all stare at me. Cam has a smirk on his face, but Josie is the first to break the silence. "Um. Is there something we need to know? What's going on between you and Holly?"

"They're fucking," Addie says, and we all whirl to face her. "What?" She shrugs. "It was obvious at Thanksgiving that you were into each other. I don't know why you're trying to be all sneaky about it."

Dammit. "Addie, we're not fucking. I'm in love with the girl. Now help me find her."

For the millionth time in my life, I'm grateful for my siblings. Addie jumps into action, leaving her drink on the bar while she takes off into the hallway to search. Josie heads for Mom to let her know what's going on, so she doesn't freak out when we all disappear.

Cam and Chris exchange a glance—the usual one they share, that says they just might regret hitching themselves to this family's shitshow—then head in different directions to search.

Where could she be?

I hear her laughter first. Not Holly's. That high-pitched, sickly-sweet fake laugh. I heard it way too many times during the year we were married, and if I never hear it again, it would be a blessing that couldn't come soon enough.

Ashley is standing in a group of men—of course—with the charm turned up high. When I tap her on the shoulder, she spins around.

"Maddox! Hi!" she squeals.

I wince, her voice already giving me a headache. "Ashley. What the fuck are you doing here?"

Her eyes are wide as she tries to look innocent. "I'm here to celebrate Judy's wedding. I'm happy for her."

"You know what? Be happy for her. I don't even care that you're here. But I will not fucking stand for you telling people you're my wife." I cross my arms over my chest.

"But I—"

"No, Ashley," I cut her off. "There's no *but*

anything, no excuses. Our marriage was a mistake. You know that as well as I do. You are no longer my wife. You never were much of a wife, anyway. How did you find out about this wedding in the first place?"

Her gaze moves quickly to one of the men in the circle, then back, but I caught it.

My cousin Brett. He's an asshole, and that's being kind. I'm about ninety percent sure Ashley slept with him while she was married to me, among the other men she fucked behind my back. He's a little weasel, and he's always had a problem with me—actually, with my sisters, too—but I never thought he would stoop so low.

"Both of you leave. Now." I look Brett directly in the eye, so he knows without a doubt that I'm talking to him.

He doesn't even argue, just sets down his beer and nods to the other guys, who are watching this unfold with varying levels of amusement.

I watch to make sure they vacate the ballroom, then look around the room to see if Holly has resurfaced. She hasn't.

Addie finds me in the hallway between the ballroom and the hotel lobby. "Hey, Maddox. I have a lead."

"Yeah?" I ask, pulling at my hair. I'll take anything.

"She booked a room. They won't tell me the number, but maybe you'll have better luck. Either way, she's here."

I give Addison a hug. "Thanks, Addie. That actually helps a lot." I look at her for a second. "Was it really that obvious at Thanksgiving?"

She grins. "Yeah. How long have you guys been a thing?"

I let out a sigh. "I... it's hard to say, really. We went out a few times before we knew Mom and Robert were together. Then she was weirded out by the future step-brother thing, but there's some other backstory. I'll leave it to her to tell you. But right now, I just need to find her."

Addie gives me a peck on the cheek. "Good luck, big brother. If you can find love, there's hope for the rest of us."

Finally, on the third try, Holly answers her phone.

"Hello?" she says, sniffling.

My heart twists. "Where are you?"

"Room 232." She sniffs again.

Thank God. "I'll be right there. Don't go anywhere." I hang up the phone and text my sisters to call off the search.

ADDIE AND JOSIE

> Found her. Everything's okay. Tell Mom we're good.

> Addie: Glad you found her. Ashley stepped in an icy puddle on the way out and her Louboutins looked ruined. I feel way too happy about this.

> Josie: I'll let Mom know. Glad you're good.

The hallway is quiet when I step off the elevator. I pause at her door, then knock.

There's a scuffling sound from inside the room. Footsteps approach the door, and then it opens.

Holly stands in the doorway with puffy eyes. She's still gorgeous even with her mascara running down her cheeks. "Maddox?"

"Can I come in?"

She opens the door a little wider, and I slip inside.

"I'm sorry, Maddox." New tears fall from red-rimmed eyes.

I hold my arms out, and she falls against me.

"This isn't your fault, babe. There's nothing to be sorry for."

She sniffles against me. "But I ran off in the middle of the reception. After I ruined their rehearsal dinner the same way."

I hold her tighter against me. "You didn't ruin anything. Ashley tried, but even she couldn't mess this up. Mom and Robert are just happy to be getting married, you know that. I'm so sorry she triggered you like that."

"I didn't believe her," she says, her voice muffled. "I know you wouldn't do that to me. But it was just like…"

"I know," I say, my hand rubbing circles on her back. "I'm sorry I didn't tell you about Ashley in the first place. I was married to her a long time ago. Right around the time my dad died. We'd been dating, and she stuck with me while he was sick. I felt like I owed her somehow, even though we were never right for one another. When it became clear that he was dying, she convinced me that we should get married so he could be there for the wedding."

Holly pulls her face out of my tux. I hope Mario can get makeup stains out. "She sounds evil."

That's an understatement. "After my dad died, Ashley kept asking about the life insurance. I think all she wanted out of me was money. I'm not even sure she was ever in love with me, honestly. Our marriage was always strained. We fought every day, and after the wedding, we barely even had sex. I'm pretty sure she was sleeping with my cousin, too."

Holly's eyes are wide. "She cheated on you?"

It feels comforting, somehow, to share that with her. No one else knows, not even Cam. But I know Holly understands what it's like.

I nod. "Pretty sure. We got divorced. We were married for just under a year, and thank God we had a prenup. But Brett, my cousin, has always had a chip on his shoulder where I'm concerned for some reason. Like he doesn't think I deserve everything I've worked for or something. And he's the one who invited Ashley to the wedding. He probably did it to fuck with me. I'm so sorry you ended up running into her."

Holly takes my hand and leads me to sit at the edge of the bed. "I'm sorry," she says softly. "I know we talked about my issues, and I thought about what you said before. I'm going to talk to someone about this. I hate that I dragged you into it."

I lace my fingers with hers. "I want to be dragged into all your stuff, Holly. No matter how messy it is. I'm all in with you."

Our eyes lock. Electricity crackles between us.

In poker, there's a point called the showdown. When all the cards are dealt, bets have been placed, and it's time to lay all your cards on the table. There's no more hiding.

This is our showdown moment.

"Remember our bet?" Holly asks.

I'm momentarily stunned. I'm ready to declare my undying love for the girl, and she wants to talk about a bet that almost ruined our relationship?

"We called that off, Holly. You didn't bring a date, but it doesn't matter. It's..."

She shakes her head again. "I need to tell you this part." She runs her tongue over her lower lip, hesitating. "I didn't bring a date. But I'm at the wedding with someone I'm in love with." She swallows, and I see a flash of vulnerability in her eyes. "I'm in love with you, Maddox. I don't know how or why, but... I don't think I can walk away from you."

26

HOLLY

I'm in love with you.

The words hang thick in the air that crackles between us. I can't breathe while I wait for him to react, to say something, anything. He sits there, still and silent, staring at me for way too long.

Finally, he blows out a breath, running a hand over his jaw. "Holly, I..."

I stand up, smacking him before he has a chance to finish dodging the question. "No, Maddox. You wanted to talk, so we're talking. I told you how I feel, if it wasn't obvious after last night. I fucking love you, but if you don't feel the same, tell me now."

I take a step toward the door when Maddox grips my upper arm, stopping me in my tracks.

He whirls me around to face him, running his free

hand over his face. "Fuck, Holly. You just caught me off-guard. I don't care about the bet. I just care about you." He holds my head, one hand on either side, his thumbs stroking my cheeks. "I love you, too."

Then his lips crash down on mine in a fiery, claiming kiss that sucks all the air from the room. Everything ceases to exist. The wedding, Ashley, the bet—everything fades away as our lips mold together.

When he pulls back, his hands still cradling my head, we're breathing hard.

"Fuck, Holly," Maddox says between breaths.

I wind my hands around him, pulling him close. "I need you, Maddox."

"Are we doing this, Holly? Like really doing this? Not a one-night stand. Not a friends with benefits thing or even just a dating thing. You're it for me, babe." Maddox's deep voice holds the slightest waver of vulnerability. Most people would miss it, but I know his voice. I know all of him.

Somewhere along the way, while I've been pushing him away, the spark between us has grown into more. So much more.

A tear threatens to fall from my eye. "You're it for me, too, Maddox," I whisper. "I'm all in."

A smile, a genuine one, stretches across his face. He grips my jaw, so tight it borders on painful but not quite, and presses his lips against mine. I part my lips when his tongue demands entry, and he deepens the kiss. Our lips still locked, Maddox walks me backwards toward the bed. He stops just as the backs of my legs hit the mattress, and if we moved any further, I'd have to bend at the knee and sit.

He presses my shoulders so I spin around, my back to him. He draws down the zipper on the back of my dress. I shrug it off and then turn back to him, clad only in my lacy white bra and matching thong.

Yeah, I wore it for him.

And his sharp intake of breath confirms that it was a good choice.

"God, Holly." His voice is choked. "Fuck, I could stare at you like this all night. Now take it the fuck off."

I unclasp the bra in the back and ease one strap down over my shoulder. "I wore it just for you," I say, letting it fall just enough that the swell of my breast peeks out.

He blows out a breath. "Are you trying to kill me, woman?"

I giggle as I slide the bra all the way off. My nipples pucker into hard peaks under his gaze. My fingers hook into the waistband of my thong, and I hesitate. The crotch is soaked with my arousal. I meet his eyes.

"Take them off, Holly," Maddox commands, his gaze darkening even further, the easy way he takes control making all my blood rush to the area between my legs.

I flush, but I pull them down and ball them up quickly, so he doesn't notice.

He holds his hand out.

"What?" I know exactly what he wants, but I'm willing to play dumb if it buys me a few minutes.

Maddox's hand doesn't waver. "Hand over the underwear. I want to see them."

Somehow, the hand holding the crumpled-up panties has hidden itself behind my back, but I manage to pull it out and hand it over.

Maddox unfolds the balled-up fabric and holds it in front of his face. Then he—oh sweet Jesus—he brings the underwear to his nose and inhales deeply.

I say nothing. What's the proper response to someone smelling your panties? He appears to be enjoying it, but do I point that out? Do I ask for them back? Do I smell his boxers?

Actually, that sounds like a terrible idea. Maddox smells amazing, don't get me wrong, but guys' underwear should never be sniffed. Let's agree on that right now.

"You smell so goddamn good, Holly. Get that

gorgeous ass on the bed for me. I want to know if you taste as good as you smell."

God, I love when Maddox goes all dirty and alpha male in the bedroom. I climb onto the bed and settle against the pillows.

Maddox stands at the foot of the bed, shrugging off his suit jacket. I watch as he undoes his shirt buttons, one by one, then pulls it off and drops the shirt on the floor. He unbuckles his belt and shoves his pants to the floor before stepping out of them. He looks damn good in a tux, but even better in his birthday suit. His cock is fully erect, tenting his boxers.

A shiver goes down my spine as I remember how that cock had felt buried deep inside me.

I need him inside me *now*.

Maddox joins me on the bed, his body above mine. He kisses me again before he sits back on his knees between my thighs. His hands gently nudge my legs wide before he bends my knees and pushes them even wider.

He takes in the view with a satisfied smirk. I'm so exposed, everything visible to Maddox.

My pussy responds by letting out a gush of moisture.

Maddox presses a soft kiss to my mound, so light that I barely feel it. His fingers trace a path along my inner thighs, pausing at the crease where my legs join my pelvis. He keeps them there while he uses his thumbs to separate my labia.

I need him to touch me. I press my hips up toward him, letting out a whine of frustration, but he holds me in place.

"Patience, babe," he murmurs.

I let out a groan and toss my head back.

Maddox's breath is hot against my body when he finally brings his head between my legs. He circles my clit with his tongue before sucking it into his mouth and biting lightly, eliciting a gasp from me.

"Fuck, Maddox," I manage.

He flattens his tongue and laps me up in long, languid strokes that have me simultaneously melting into the bed and coiling in a tense ball of muscle. He keeps going, varying his speed and his angles just enough that it brings me right to the edge and keeps me there.

I'm so close to exploding. "Maddox. I want you inside me," I gasp as his tongue presses harder against my clit.

He picks his head up, his dark stare burning into my eyes as he shakes his head. "Don't rush me, Holly. We have all night. And I plan to enjoy every inch of you. This time, I want you dripping wet from your orgasm before I fuck you, baby. So you're going to come hard for me while I eat your sweet pussy. Got it?"

Oh my God. I've never been with someone who can talk dirty like Maddox can. His words make every bit of blood that's not already pooling between my legs go straight to my core.

"Got it, babe?" Maddox says, a little more sharply.

I nod, my lower lip caught between my teeth as I try to hold in a groan.

Maddox's hand comes down on my inner thigh with a sharp slap that's more surprising than painful. "Got it, babe? Use your words. I want to hear that gorgeous voice."

"Fuck! Yes. God. Fuck. Yes, Maddox."

A smile spreads across his face. "Good girl. Hold on."

With the last words, he slides one long finger inside me, pressing up against my pussy wall as he dives back in, flicking his tongue over my clit. I groan out as he replaces his one finger with two, then adds a third. He drives them into me while his tongue traces patterns over my most sensitive areas.

"Come for me, Holly," he murmurs against me, curling his fingers inside me to press against my g-spot. He pulls my clit into his mouth and sucks hard while my pussy spasms around his fingers.

I manage to say his name amidst the moans as my body shudders with a climax.

He barely gives me time to come down from my orgasm before he's rolling on a condom and notching himself at my entrance.

"Holly. Look at me." His voice is deep and commanding in a way that I've only ever heard in the bedroom. His usual confident, easygoing manner transforms into a man who knows how to take control.

I force my eyes open to meet his gaze. His pupils are so dilated with lust that his eyes look almost black. A muscle in his jaw twitches.

"Last chance, babe. We do this, we're all in. If you're not serious, let me know. Right. Fucking. Now." His voice is strained from the effort of holding himself still.

This makes me fall in love with him even more, if that's even possible. "I'm sure, Maddox. I'm all in here. You're what I need."

We're lying together, sated. It feels so good to just *be* with Maddox. I roll to my side, facing him, and trace circles on his chest with my finger.

I feel amazing, so complete, but then something pops into my head, and I frown.

"How are you doing, baby?" he asks, smoothing his hand over my hair.

I let out a sigh. "I'm good. So good. I just had a work thought."

He shifts so he's on his side too, both of us facing one another. "What's going on?"

"It's Julio. I've told you about him, right? He's eight, and he's been in the system since he was two. I've been his case worker since I finished grad school, so a little over three years. He's this amazing little kid with a shitty situation. It just tugs at my heartstrings every time I see him." I run a hand over my face.

"What's going on with Julio?" Maddox asks, ever the patient listener.

God, he'd be a great shrink, wouldn't he? There's something about the way he listens, letting you speak without interrupting, and the way he prompts you to finish your story before he adds his own thoughts.

I swallow hard. "He's been with a nice older couple for a while, but they told me early in November that they were going to be retiring, that they couldn't take foster kids anymore."

Maddox nods, his brow furrowing. "So, where does that leave Julio?"

Tears prick at my eyes as I shrug. "Nowhere. That's the problem. I've been trying to find him a place to go because they can't keep him after the end of December. That's in a week, and it's not like anything ever gets done the week between Christmas and New Year's. I just feel like I failed him. He's going to have to go to a group home."

Maddox's brow creases. "Did you ask my mom?"

"Ask your mom what?" I have no idea what this has to do with Julio.

"If she can take Julio." He shrugs slightly.

I smile. "Aw, that's really sweet, Maddox. But there's all sorts of red tape and things for foster placements. She'd have to be approved as a foster parent, and that can take a while."

Maddox stares at me. "She's been a foster parent for years. She and my dad have fostered tons of kids over the years."

I sit up straight, pulling the covers to my armpits. "She's *what?*" How did I not know this? She's in a different county, so obviously she wouldn't be on my list of foster parents, but it's never come up in conversation.

Maddox nods sheepishly. "I can't believe we never talked about this. I think I was so wrapped up in you and me that I didn't even think to tell you about our family. Or maybe I've just shared so much with you that I forgot that I hadn't told you already. All of us were adopted from the foster system. Addie, Josefina, and me. Addie and I when we were about three or four. Josie when she was closer to nine. Didn't you wonder why I have one redheaded sister and a Mexican sister?"

I guess I hadn't really noticed, honestly. I'm used to blended families, so it doesn't stand out, and I just thought Josie was more tan than Addie. I figured she had their dad's coloring.

And no one told me her real name was Josefina.

It all starts to make a little more sense now, the things I didn't pick up on earlier. Why there aren't any pictures of any of the Anderson kids before about age three or four. Why there are periods of time without any photos, because you're not allowed to share pictures of foster kids who are still in the system. How Judy can manage conflict without batting an eye or raising her voice.

Maddox is sitting up now, too. "She still takes in kids, mostly emergency short-term placements. She hasn't had one in a while, probably because she's been busy with your dad. But if there's a kid in need, she'd be the first to open her home to him. Ask her."

I'm still searching for words as Maddox takes out his phone and calls someone.

"Hey, Mom. Sorry to bother you. I'm with Holly. You know she's a caseworker with DHS in Philadelphia, right? Anyway, she wanted to talk with you about something. Hang on." He holds the phone out to me.

My eyes are wide as I scrape my jaw off the floor and take the phone from Maddox. "Hi, Judy? I'm so sorry to bother you on your wedding night. I want to talk to you about a little guy named Julio."

27

HOLLY

Neither Maddox nor I brought extra clothes, so we do the walk of shame in our crumpled clothes from last night.

Except for my underwear. Maddox still won't give that back.

He got a ride here with his sister, so he drives my car carefully back to the city. The snow blankets everything in a silent wonderland, but the plows have been out all night, so the roads aren't too bad. He even manages to find street parking and parallel parks my little Corolla like an expert right in front of my building.

I'm never moving my car. I'll never find a parking spot this close again. Rideshares and buses it is from now on.

Maddox follows me as I walk into the lobby, kicking snow off my ballet slippers and trying to thaw my toes.

"Aren't you going home?" I ask, confused. I mean, I want him here. I'd want to be with him all the time if I could.

Maybe not when he's picking his toe jam. But all the other times, definitely.

And don't tell me he doesn't do that. All men do, according to JJ, and she knows a lot of men.

"Not yet," he says, following me into the elevator.

This might be the first time I've brought a man home. JJ will have a field day, what with our rumpled clothes and my obvious sex hair.

I push the key into the lock and turn it, then shove with my hip to open the door.

My jaw falls open.

Maddox steps inside the apartment, coming to stand next to me as he closes the door behind us.

"Merry Christmas!" JJ hops out from her bedroom, dressed like an elf.

"JJ?" I ask. "Did you do all of this?" She doesn't even celebrate Christmas, other than when I've dragged her to my dad's house. Usually, we follow her Jewish heritage and get Chinese food on Christmas Eve.

She shrugs, the bell on her elf hat jingling. "Well, I did. But it was all Maddox's idea."

"Just some Christmas magic for you, babe," he murmurs in my ear.

It *is* magic. There's a tree in one corner, filled with lights that blink on and off in all different colors, and candy canes hang from the branches. There's tinsel on everything, and more Christmas lights are strung around the room. There are snowflake stickers on the windows.

Under the tree, there's one present wrapped in a small box.

I turn to Maddox, my voice choked with emotion. "Thank you. This means so much to me."

He gives me a hug, brushing his lips over mine. "We're going to make every Christmas magical for you from now on, Holly. You deserve it."

"Open your present!" JJ demands, interrupting our kiss.

I break away from Maddox, giggling. "Jeez, JJ. Don't you have your own man to entertain right now?"

She waves a dismissive hand in the air. "He had to work. Open it!"

I cross the apartment and pick up the box from

beneath the tree. It's wrapped in plaid paper, with a gift tag on the front.

Merry Christmas, baby.

There's no indication who it's from.

I look at JJ. "Is this from you?"

She shakes her head, and I look at Maddox.

He just winks. "Maybe it's from Santa."

I roll my eyes, but I tear the paper off and open the box. There's a key sitting there.

I look to Maddox. "Is this to your..." I don't want to assume he got me a key to his place, but what else could it open?

He shakes his head, but he's smiling. "Not to my place, babe. To yours. Ours, hopefully. I got your dad to sell you the house. You have to sign some papers and you won't get the deed until after New Year's, but it's all yours."

28

MADDOX

TWO MONTHS LATER

If I was in a position to get married in my sixties, you'd better believe I'm going on a honeymoon that lasts weeks, if not months. I sure as shit wouldn't be skipping it altogether to invite a kid into my home.

I suppose that just means that my mom and Robert are better people than I am, or at least that they've had enough experience in their lifetimes to be able to prioritize more effectively. They decided to cancel their honeymoon entirely, foregoing wine tasting in Napa to take in Julio. It's been almost two months since he moved in, and I think Holly might have some serious competition when it comes to who loves Julio the most, because Robert and my mom are enamored.

He really is the cutest little guy. He's living in Addison's old room, which has been completely redone in shades of dark blue with a space theme.

If I'm being honest, it looks much better than how it did before, with posters plastered all over the walls with pictures of male celebrities—the ones who were "hot," according to Addie—and animals. Addie, being Addie, doesn't care at all that her room has been taken over. Of the three Anderson kids, she's the most easy-going by far.

I pull into the driveway and put the car in park behind a Subaru, rounding the car to open the passenger side door for Holly. She steps out, her short high heels tapping on the asphalt.

Kitten heels. That's right. That's what she called them. The name makes no sense to me. Just call them short high heels. Then we all know what we're talking about.

"Is this weird?" Holly asks, chewing on her bottom lip.

I shake my head. "Not at all. We're visiting our parents and their foster kid."

She doesn't look reassured. "Whose cars are these? Are Addison and Josie and Chris here?"

I shrug. "No idea. Let's go in and we'll find out."

Holly still looks stressed as fuck, but she takes my hand and lets me lead her up to the door.

"It's weird to visit my dad at your mom's house," she whispers.

I ring the doorbell. "It's his house too, now. And it's not any weirder than when your dad visits us at his old house. Haven't you done a home visit for Julio?"

"I've seen him, but not as his social worker. I had to give his case to one of my colleagues. Conflict of interest and all that." A flash of pain makes its way across her face, and I squeeze her into my side.

The door opens to reveal a small boy with dark hair and light brown skin. He's wearing what must be brand-new Nike sneakers, a royal blue sweatshirt with the NASA logo, and the biggest smile I've ever seen.

"Miss Holly!" he cries out, jumping into her arms.

Holly is wearing an identical expression as she folds him into a hug. "Julio, it's so good to see you! I've missed you so much, kiddo. Are you having fun here? Do you like Judy and my dad? Robert?"

She releases him, and Julio steps back, nodding. "They're so cool. I love it here." A worried expression crosses his face, his tiny brows knitting together. "I hope I don't have to leave."

"That's not something you need to worry about, Julio. Remember?" Judy appears behind him, placing her hands on his small shoulders. "Come in, you guys. It's good to see you."

We make our way into the house, each of us receiving a hug from my mom. As it turns out, all of the Anderson kids are here. Addie is curled in an armchair, and Josie and Chris are cuddled together on one of the couches, looking happier than I've seen Josie in a long time. We were all here for Thanksgiving —most of us—but it feels different today. More cohesive, like we're one big family. We are, I guess. It's been just mom and us kids for so long, but we feel complete now.

Mom drops onto the couch opposite us, with Julio sandwiched between her and Robert. He looks squished, but happy. I glance at Holly. She's taking it in too, a smile wide across her face.

"So. Kids. We have some news," Mom starts.

Holly nudges me.

"As you know, Julio has been living with us for a couple months. We love him dearly, as you can imagine."

Holly gives Julio a big smile and a wink.

"So even though Robert and I are old,"—she pauses to smile at him when he smacks her playfully— "we have moved through the red tape and have finalized plans to adopt Julio. Congratulations, kids. You have a new little brother."

The reactions are predictable, at least.

Addie jumps up and squeals.

Holly runs over to Julio and envelops him in another hug.

Josie smiles politely, but it looks like a real smile as Chris squeezes her tighter.

I wait for Holly to release Julio before I step over to him. I squat down, bringing my large frame down so we're face to face. "Welcome to the family, man. Hug or high five?"

Julio's eyes widen at being given a choice. He looks to Robert, who just gives him a smile and a slight nod.

"High five," Julio says quietly.

I hold up my hand and wait for him to plant his fist against it, which he does with surprising force for a little kid. I give him a smile before I retreat to my seat.

As the noise dies down—mostly Addie's noise, as usual—I clear my throat.

"I, uh, have some news, too," I say. Fuck, is this how Mom and Robert felt a few minutes ago? Completely on the spot?

I clear my throat again. "So. Holly and I are..."

Addison claps her hands and lets out a tiny squeal.

I scowl at her. "Jesus, woman. Let me finish."

She holds her hands up in mock surrender.

"As I was saying. Holly and I are moving in together." I wait for their reaction.

Addie looks at Josie. Mom looks at Robert. None of them appear the least bit surprised. They seem confused actually, like this is old news to them.

The only one looking at me is Julio, who looks pretty damn judgmental for an eight-year-old. I watch as he tugs on Robert's sleeve and whispers something in his ear.

Robert's face creases in a smile as he listens to Julio. He erupts in a fit of laughter. "Do I think he's good enough for Holly?"

Wait. Fuck. The kid thinks I'm not good enough?

Holly starts laughing too, and then the girls all join in.

Robert rises from his feet and crosses the room to stand in front of me. "Well, son. It seems you took my advice."

Holly's eyes widen as her father grips me in a quick hug before returning to his seat.

"My dad knew?" she asks, her gaze darting between Robert and me.

I nod. "I called him for advice, back when you weren't sure about me. Asked if it would be weird to date his daughter. Think it worked out okay?"

Holly looks around at the smiling faces. "I guess so."

I dig in my pocket. "Now. I know we called off the bet, but I still feel like I owe you a win, because you ended up at the wedding with a man you were in love with. One who loved you back one hundred percent."

She nods, but her brow creases in confusion. "You already donated so much to that organization I told you about. You don't owe me anything."

I pull something out of my pocket, sliding off the couch to rest on one knee in front of Holly. "I do. And I'm hoping this might be an acceptable prize." I hold out the diamond solitaire and hold my breath.

Her smile doesn't fade, but her brow wrinkles. "Um. Maddox?"

"Oh. Right." I give her another wink. "Will you marry me?"

The smile that spreads across her face is one of the most beautiful things I've ever seen.

"I love you, Maddox. Of course I'll marry you."

I slide the ring onto her finger and step back as she admires it, and as Addison, Josie, and my mom gather around her.

I squeeze her tight. It feels so good, so right to have her here in my arms, surrounded by our family.

Holly pulls back, her eyes bright. She hugs me again, and this time, Julio buries himself between us.

I didn't even see the little ninja get up from the couch. Sneaky little thing.

"Miss Holly, I'm so happy for you!" His muffled voice comes from between us. "Can I be in your wedding?"

Holly laughs. "Of course, Julio. I'm not your caseworker anymore, but you're my brother. I'd love for you to be in my wedding."

Even Josie gives Holly a big hug. Maybe Holly managed to break through Josie's walls.

But Josie's smile doesn't fade when she releases Holly. If anything, it widens as she looks at Chris. "So, if we're all sharing news, we have some, too."

Chris stands up to hold her hand.

Josie beams as Chris puts her hands over Josie's belly. "We're pregnant. Twins. The IVF worked."

Another round of cheers erupts from everyone but Julio, who's asking my mom what IVF is.

Robert taps me on the shoulder as the girls take turns embracing one another, happy tears in all of their eyes. "Congratulations, son. I'd say welcome to the family, but..." He sweeps his hand toward my mom.

I just smile.

EPILOGUE

ONE YEAR LATER

Holly

I don't want a big wedding. Just a quick ceremony with family and friends, no frills.

Honestly, I'd be good with no wedding at all, but Judy insisted.

We've got the officiant settled, the venue, the food. We're sitting at our kitchen table planning our honeymoon now, trying to figure out how I can take a week off so we can go to Italy.

I check my email again and let out a whoop of excitement. "He approved it!"

Maddox's head pops up from the laptop in front of him. "He did?"

I nod frantically. "He did! My vacation is officially

approved, signed off by the boss. Book the flights now before he changes his mind!"

Maddox clicks away on his computer for a few minutes. "And... done. We're booked for flights to Rome and a week touring Rome and Florence."

I clap my hands. The wedding is in two months. The honeymoon is the last big thing to check off on the to-do list. Now it's on to the fun things, like the final fittings of the wedding dress that Judy helped me pick out.

I meet Maddox's gaze across the table and grin.

Maddox

I finalize our nonrefundable flights. I can't wait to marry her. Thank fuck she finally agreed to be with me. I thought getting her to marry me would be the biggest hurdle, but once she agreed to date me, everything came together. I can't even remember what life was like before her.

I slip out my phone and tap on the calendar to put the dates of our honeymoon into the schedule. I pull up the date we're planning to fly out of Philadelphia and pause.

"Oh. Crap."

Holly's head pops up from where she's tapping on her phone. "Crap what? What's wrong?"

I tug on the back of my neck. "I forgot that I told Cam I'd do this cruise ship thing with him. He got a gig dealing blackjack and poker on a cruise ship. We've been on some list for a year, and he got a call a few months ago that they wanted us to work spring break week. It was supposed to be a good paycheck, but mostly just fun. We're supposed to leave two days after our wedding. I kind of forgot all about it. But it's at the same time as our honeymoon."

Holly lifts her brow. "You can still go if you want. We can change the timing of things on our end."

Yeah, delay marrying the girl of my dreams so I can spend a week on a cruise ship, sharing a tiny cabin with Cam and his smelly socks? Hard pass.

"I'll tell Cam I can't go. I'll find someone to go with him instead, so he doesn't have to worry about it. He's pretty chill. He'll be okay." I nod, convincing myself.

"If you're sure, that would be good. The flight is nonrefundable, isn't it?"

I nod. "Yeah. That was my bad. But I'll make sure he has someone to go with him. He's taking the breakup with Ellie really hard, more than usual, so it makes me think this breakup is for real. Not like the hundred other times they've broken up, only to get back together a week later. I don't need him stewing about that while he's trapped at sea."

Holly grins. "True. Maybe we can hook him up with one of my friends. I'd say JJ, but I'm pretty sure she's headed down the aisle with Justin any day now. They've been inseparable for about as long as we have."

I smile at her as I start texting, looking for someone to be my substitute for this cruise.

CARD SHARKS

> Hey, either of you guys interested in dealing poker and blackjack for a week with Cam? Cruise ship, should be sweet.

Miller: Ehh I'm out. I get seasick.

Blake: Depends when it is, but I'm pretty booked up, so probably not.

I text him the dates. He's got plans. Of course.

Fuck. Of course those assholes can't help out. I blow out a breath of frustration.

"No luck?" Holly asks, leaning over my shoulder.

I shake my head. "No. Miller and Blake are out. I need someone who knows what they're doing, but it also has to be someone who can either take a week off work or who doesn't have set hours." And unfortunately, people like that don't grow on trees.

Holly tilts her head to the side in thought as she taps her chin. "What about Addison? She's a teacher, right? See if her spring break matches with the dates."

I open my mouth to protest, but then close it again. If Addie has the week off, she might be my only option. She knows how to play and deal most card games, and I'm sure she'd love a free vacation. I don't love the idea of her going on a cruise, but Cam could keep an eye on her, keep her out of trouble. I send a text before I can think better of it.

ADDISON

> When's your spring break? If it's the week of April 14, any interest in a cheap cruise? Or free. I'm desperate, I'll cover it for you.

She texts back almost immediately, a string of emojis that I interpret as excitement.

.   .   .

I let out a sigh of relief and gather Holly to me. One crisis solved. I'm sure another one is just around the corner, but with Holly at my side, we can take on anything.

Find JJ and Justin's story in <u>Rolling The Dice</u>!
This FREE novella is available exclusively to Newsletter subscribers. Get yours here or sign up at katecampfield.com.

Find Cam and Addie's story in Betting on Love Book
2:
Letting it Ride

After my last break up, I know better than to gamble on love. And going after my best friend's younger sister is a sure way to lose it all.

At thirty-four, I should be focused on buying my first house and funding my 401k–not dragging my best friend on a cruise to escape reality. But after a brutal breakup, this vacation is the only bright spot in my otherwise crappy life.

Not on my cruise itinerary? My best friend's sister showing up...or gambling my heart with her in the worst rebound fling decision of my life. I've known her so long she may as well be my sister, too, but between our natural chemistry, protecting her from sleazy guys, and making sure she doesn't fall overboard, I'm starting to think dirty thoughts about her that I know I shouldn't.

It's all I can do to just get through this week at sea. But when our cruise ends abruptly with us stranded, forcing us to work together to get out of this mess, I'm not sure how much longer I can fight these feelings... even if it costs me my best friend.

Fans of Lucy Score and Pippa Grant will love this steamy brother's-best-friend romantic comedy!

AUTHOR'S NOTE

One of the children Holly cares for as a social worker is a baby who was surrendered in a Safe Haven Baby Box. While you can surrender an infant at any fire department, police station or hospital in most states, these boxes are safe ways for an unwanted baby to be given up, no questions asked and no contact with anyone.

You can find a list of available Safe Haven Baby Boxes at https://shbb.org/. Please consider asking your local government to support the addition of more of these boxes to help save infants and get them into the arms of a family that is ready to care for them.

Kate crafts fast-paced, spicy contemporary romance and romantic comedy. Growing up as one of five kids, she mastered the art of escaping into fictional worlds, often by "borrowing" her mom's Nora Roberts books. These days, when she's not busy creating her own swoon-worthy tales, she's devouring Meghan Quinn and Elsie Silver novels like they're the hottest gossip at a family reunion.

When she's not embroiling her characters in yet another laugh-out-loud disaster, you can usually find her surrounded by animals or with her nose buried in a spicy read. Her pets behave as if they're the real brains behind her stories, but Kate remains unconvinced—though she admits they do have a knack for comedic timing.

Follow Kate on social media and sign up for her newsletter to hear Ollie's life advice and book reviews. Disclaimer: Ollie is a German Shepherd. His judgment is questionable. Kate strongly advises against following his advice—unless you're a dog, in which case, bark away.

9 781962 697057